Samuel Lilienthal, Joseph Benedict Buchner

Morbus Brighti

Samuel Lilienthal, Joseph Benedict Buchner

Morbus Brighti

ISBN/EAN: 9783337197780

Printed in Europe, USA, Canada, Australia, Japan

Cover: Foto ©Andreas Hilbeck / pixelio.de

More available books at **www.hansebooks.com**

BY

JOSEPH BUCHNER,

DOCTOR OF PHILOSOPHY AND MEDICINE, MEMBER OF MANY LEARNED
SOCIETIES AND ACADEMIES IN EUROPE AND AMERICA,
PRESIDENT OF THE HOMŒOPATHIC HOSPITAL IN MUNICH,
PROFESSOR AT THE LUDOVICO-MAXIMILIANEA.

Non cuivis contingit adire Corinthum.

Hor. Ep. I. 17. 36.

TRANSLATED BY

SAMUEL LILIENTHAL, M. D.

BOERICKE & TAFEL,

NEW YORK, 145 Grand St.   PHILADELPHIA, 635 Arch St.
PHILADELPHIA, 48 North 9th St.   BALTIMORE, 19 N. Eutaw St.
SAN FRANCISCO, 234 Sutter Street.

————

1872.

Some of our readers might object to the title *"Morbus Brighti,"* and not *"Brightii,"* but as DR. BUCHNER is responsible for the title of his book, I did not feel at liberty to alter it.

S. L.

TRANSLATOR'S PREFACE.

Home, sweet Home!! After 35 years' residence in our adopted fatherland, the heart still yearns after our Alma Mater, and it became a work of love for us, to translate a book, which has for its author a teacher of our old and still-beloved Ludovico-Maxmilianea.

But a far more cogent reason is, that Buchner's Morbus Brighti is by far the best and exhausting monograph, ever written on this subject. He treads no barren ground, but investigates everything himself, and as a scientific Homœopath he studies in his therapeutics the reasons, why each remedy produces such and such symptoms, and ergo why in curative cases its beneficial effect must follow with mathematical precision.

Oh! that we had more such workers, or rather that the many eminent men, our school can boast of, could gain time enough from their daily work, to perform the same scientific labor on every remedy. Give us a physiological and histological Materia

Medica, and the general acceptance of Homœopathy by all schools must be the necessary consequence.

Our thanks are due to Dr. Mary H. Everett, for having aided us in the revision of the manuscript. German authors write in so heavy and entangled periods that it is frequently difficult to render it in good old English, and we ask the pardon of our readers for the shortcomings, which after all are apt to creep in.

Our work is done. May it spur us on, to complete, what Buchner has left undone.

New York, July, 1872.

                    S. LILIENTHAL, M. D.

PREFACE BY THE AUTHOR.

Thirty years ago we offered our first mite to homœopathic literature. Since that time, as it is with most homœopathic physicians, our daily practice took up all our time, and by the midnight lamp once and a while we hurriedly wrote an article for a medical journal on this, a favorite study of ours. At last this monograph was finished. It contains dry facts, based on physiology and chemistry, shows the deficiencies under which we still labor, but gives in full everything, which has proved itself valuable in practice. We have never been afraid, to give and to hold on to our own opinions in opposition to generally adopted views, but everywhere we give our reasons.

We are not egotistic enough to consider our little work perfect, and it would give us the greatest satisfaction, when men like J. C. Muller, Eidherr, Neidhart and others, could spare so much time from their practice, to render by further studies our little book obsolete and if younger men, who must be educated to such labors and who do not grow wild like Artemisia vulgaris, could be found, to fill up the gaps in our Materia Medica. We have educated with a good deal of loss of time some men, who have become an honor to Homœopathy. Durate, says Virgil, let none forget the future on account of the present. The fruits of the tree which we plant, our children will enjoy.

We do not ask for rockets from our critics, but so much practical experience, that they have already treated the syphilitic form of Morbus Brighti and that they supply everything, which is liable to censure, by making it better, for which we will thank them with all our heart.

DR. J. BUCHNER.

Munich.

INTRODUCTION.

The fact, that among chronic patients a very large proportion die of Bright's Disease, as many at least as from Tuberculosis, has induced me to write this monograph and to designate the standpoint, from which alone a rational and exact therapia is possible.

Rokitansky justly remarks, that pathological anatomy is the theoretical basis for all medical knowledge. Pathological anatomy in its perfection is only physiological pathology, just as Materia Medica is the physiology of the action of remedies. Another and most important desideratum for the *practical physician*, is consequently the action of remedies on the healthy; for every one who has to act, be he mechanist, chemist, or physician, ought to know the powers with which he acts, experimentally and physiologically, locally and specifically, may he treat on the homœopathic or antipathic principle; for many remedies act both ways, like Opium, and may be applied in different doses according to the principle of similarity and partial similarity or contrariety, as Natrum sulph. in gonorrhœa, Kali jod. etc., all narcotica even in a threefold relation: positive, negative and undulating.

Pathological anatomy, chemistry and microscopy have just as little value for the physician, who has no principles to guide him, and cannot draw proper conclusions, as the forest and thick undergrowth of the physiological effects of remedies for him, who cannot select the keynotes of a remedy and prescribes e. g. Anacardium in syphilitic eczema. Our aim is, to study the differential diagnosis of Morbus Brighti in a scientific and practical manner, and to demonstrate how it can be homœopathically cured; how far we succeed, every candid observer may judge for himself; though it may have no bearing on the great importance of pathological physiology or physiological pathology, still for the practical physician we consider " provings of the healthy " the great desideratum. Not only solitary learned men, but entire societies have since Haller acknowledged the truth of this assertion, but its execution remained difficult, because the physiological effects of medicines are not so readily found, as those of the diseases, and especially because in our age of skepsis the real relations between remedy and disease could not be digested, and far less individualized. Even homœopathic physicians, blinded by materialistic proofs, forgot the old maxim nil admirari, semper res est una, and burst full of admiration in New York and Prague, whereas the present regular school stands on the negative, unable to create anything positive, having no principle to guide them, and their greatest glory, pathological anatomy, possesses no ideas on which to base therapeutics; they intend to go by their experience, which has and will render all medicine uncouth and trivial.

MORBUS BRIGHTI.

Superficially considered symptoms and their causes appear equivalent to organic alterations ; but thus tho knowledge of the adjectives of the disease, Grauvogl's constitution, becomes difficult, as it can only be safely determined from the subjective phenomena. We therefore take the symptoms collectively, the organic lesions in their unity. A consideration e. g. of the different exudations in lungs and pleura, will explain my meaning. Although the exudation is the essence of the inflammation, the quality of it does not depend on the disease, but on the state of the patient, and thus forms a further link in our diagnosis, of great importance in the selection of the remedy and which we call the adjectivism of the disease. In the various forms of renal degeneration the same relation takes place, the latter often is as right to left, all of which has to be taken into account. Apparently similar states, which from an anatomical standpoint might be declared identical, are clinically considered extremely different. Inflammations in fibrinous, anæmic patients, run a different course from what they do in albuminous, gelatinous ones; every form therefore needs different remedies.

A homœopathic physician must diagnose far more accurately, than he, who treats on a general plan, and prescribes organ-remedies or specifics; we *must* find the homœopathic remedy, a unity ideal, real and principal. The modalities of the disease are important and allow us with more ease to find the object of the disease, but they do not form the adjectivum, being only a part of it, which is composed of the patient, his objective symptoms and their causes.

Our chief labor consists therefore, in rendering serviceable to practice every progress of theoretical science, by establishing a differential diagnosis of the disease and of the idiopathic remedy, which can only be done by the physiological experiment with remedies. We start from life, others from death. Will we finally meet?

It is clear in relation to the dose, that only a certain one can be absolutely the right one, all the disputes of high or low dilutions are without any scientific value. In diseases with so deeply penetrating organic lesions in different organs, as in Morbus Brighti, we prefer the lower dilutions.

HISTORY OF THE DISEASE.

It is the duty of the history of science, with our present acquisitions to affirm or to disprove the theories of the past.

Hippocrates mentions a dropsy, emanating from the lumbar region; *Aetius* and *Avicenna* dropsies from renal diseases. *Horatius* knew a dirus hydrops. The old physicians, who began to make more frequent dissections and used the results therefrom for their diagnosis, knew as well as we do, several forms of nephritis and called them by adjectives, which were of importance for the mediate diagnosis, and carried the hydrops back more or less clearly to nephritic diseases, as *Helmont*: verus hydrops ascites est in renibus. *Morgagni* also mentions an ascites from renal alterations, also *Bonet*. *F. Hoffmann* distinguished inflammation of the renal substance and its membranes, as simple and calcular nephritis, although at that time the tendency of medicine was chemical. The expression *typhus urinosus* is as old as it is expressive.

Cotugno, 1770, and still more *Cruickshanc*, 1798, recognized albumen in the urine of dropsical patients, and other physicians confirmed it and divided hydrops into that with coagulable and non-coagulable urine, *Blackall*, 1813, which is of importance for prognosis as well as for therapeutics. Wells demonstrated albumen in hydrops after scarlatina and showed, that frequent pains in the renal region and material alterations in the parenchyma accompany coagulable urine.

With the practical realization of the microscope the doctrine of nephritis gained a new basis, and *Richard Bright*, 1807, was the first who taught with precision, that many dropsies are based on a peculiar alteration of the kidneys, and that this alienation can be recognised by the quantity of albumen in the urine. *Bostock* made chemical examinations of the urine and found alterations, which are simultaneously present in the blood. *Robinson* and especially *Christison*, 1839, wrote after Bright on granular degeneration of the kidneys in its acute or chronic state, and many English physicians, like *Hamilton*, affirmed the discovery, whereas in France they wrote on ṇephritis albuminosá. *Osborne* first noticed the suppression of cutaneous action as a cause of the disease. *Rayer* considered the disease as a peculiar form of nephritis and as albuminous ; *M. Solon*, 1838, lays great stress on the organic alterations ; *Bequerel*, 1841, (Hypertrophy of the Malpighian bodies,) *Rokitanksy*, *Hansen*, *Malmsten*, *Rees*, *Johnson :* nephritis desquamativa acuta et chronica, etc. *Henle* first demonstrated the fibrinous cylinders. *Reinhardt* pointed out the disease as a specific inflammatory process, whose fibrinous exudation shows no tendency to organization, a diffuse croupous nephritis.

Frerichs wrote the best work, worthy of German diligence. These and other physicians as *Hammernik*, *Virchow :* nephritis albuminosa parenchymatosa, *Heller*, *Kletzinsky*, *Buhl*, *Quaglio*, each in his peculiar sphere, enlarged the knowledge of the disease, of its forms and of its primary and secondary organic alterations.

Skoda, like us, does not acknowledge a croupy form of Bright's disease. The material before us shows, how long and laborious the way of such an investigation is, ars longa, vita brevis, and how difficult it is to render it useful in practice. To give full importance to the pathological states, we must first study its physiology.

DIGNITY OF THE RENAL FUNCTION.

In order to value fully the consequences of nutritive disturbances in the kidneys, let us study the organic question of the activity of the kidneys. If we consider the daily aqueous excretion of the organismus at 80 ounces, 30 ounces of it are renal secretion, and what we must here especially consider, the urea, as the representative of the used up azote. The kidney is the chief actor for the wholesale excretion of azote, as the other azote exhalations from the lungs and skin are only returns of the atmospheric nitrogen gas, and are not worthy of any consideration in comparison with the urine, and experience shows, that a grown up person discharges a quantity of nitrogen in the urine corresponding to the quantity introduced. With an ordinary diet one ounce urea is daily discharged, representing 220 grs. azote, even when the food simply passes through the organismus, without any such secretory interchange taking place, or without the export of urea ceasing from want of importing it with the food, which, even admitting a præformation of urea in the blood, leaves its chief formation to the activity of the kidneys. Now, if the kidneys from whatever cause are unable to produce normal secretion, and at the same time discharge useful matter like albumen, and leave in the organism that which is useless, like nitrogenous bodies, then the blood as feeder of the tissues and mediator of all nutrition, finds it as impossible with a surplus of nitrogen to retain its organic functional

2*

integrity, as do some solid organs, like the spinal cord; we must study such a procedure not only in Bright's disease, but especially in its uræmic forms; in its chemical, as well as in its functional relations.

Physiology shows, that all circumstances which prevent the discharge of blood from the kidneys, increase the density of the urine, proving, that the vascular coils of the kidneys are the real organs of filtration for the urine; in a similar manner an over-filling of the urinary canals with fluid, exercises a pressure on the blood vessels of the coil, preventing secretion; furthermore, the to and fro motion, which forwards the discharge of the excreted solution to the urinary canals, increases thus the functional ability of the vascular coils, through which the so-frequently mentioned mechanical side pressure loses in importance.

It is certain, that albumen appears in the urine, when the pressure of the arterial or venous blood is greatly increased, and that under the usual pressure albumen is never found.

We might also mention Hessling's supposition, that the mixture emanating from the vascular coils loses its albumen by new-formations, also *Wittich;* *Heynsius* on the contrary affirms, that the renal capillaries on account of the acidity of the renal tissue, which reacts equally sour in man and beast (whereon we base the chemical examination in hæmorrhage of the urinary organs) are impassable for albumen. It is not yet settled what influences predominate in the kidneys in their ability of oxidation, they are probably partly nervous, partly the quantity of oxygen in the blood and body, and whose deficiency with its sequels we see most clearly in cholera. The more nitrogen, the less oxygen, as in croup the poisoning by carbon, in diphtheria both, therefore in severe cases Bright's disease. We must also mention the experiments of *Kierulf*, where albuminuria showed itself after aqueous injection in the circulation of animals and the kidneys presented the first stage of Bright's disease. Gallic acid acted in the same way: *Kuehne;* albumen of chickens injected in the blood passes unaltered in the urine: *Stockvis*. *Thiersch's* metabolic matter. We might put it down as an axiom: whatever acts paralysing on the blood-corpuscles, whatever renders them incapable to fix oxygen may produce Bright's disease.

The cellular layer of the urinary canals, the epithelium, is very easily destroyed, and we therefore mostly perceive only cells bereft of their globular surrounding. The glandular cells, which influence the product, become flat toward the capsule of Mueller and pass over into tesselated epithelium, which lines the capsule without continuing in the malpighian tufts. It is said that this epithelium secretes the uric salts. Those who suppose the tufts provided with epithelial cells, describe them as flat cells closely adhering to the windings, which like all tessellated cells are incapable of great material exchange, as the globulars of the glandular cells, which morbidly affected produce albuminous urine. We would also remark that the lumen of the straight urinary canals of the pyramids appears wider, on account of the smallness of their cells, than the lumen of the twisted and turning cortical tubuli; fatty corpuscles in them must be considered as detritus, forming itself from the used up glandular epithelium.

To the physiological function of the kidney we may join the neglected doctrine of the excretory ways of matter, not nutritive but remedial, so often and in such large quantities applied by physician and layman, that the organismus need taking more care for their excretion than for the supposed curative effects. We distinguish among them *permeating*, e. g. the coloring matter of black cherries, but not that of rheum, which relaxed the intestinal muscles in the same degree as the tubuli and tufts of the kidney, *primary*, as Canth., and *secondary specific* remedies, as Arsen. Although we cannot speak in such rough cases of a practically useful observation, but only from a supplementary one, still the excretory organs of remedies are needed to give us a base for their localization and their specific deposition. The following facts are so far proved : *Oxalic acid*, internally given, is always found in combination with lime in the well known microscopic octohedral form after a few hours and calcarea oxalica is produced by all beverages containing carbonic acid (Champagne,) after the use of rotten potatoes, sorrel or phloridzin, also tartaric acid (Woehler), tartaric Antimon.? the tartaric acid of Moselle wines which ought never be given to patients with diseased kidneys, gallic acid in 20 minutes (Woehler), tannic acid from Catechu

in 20 minutes (Mitcherlich), succinic acid, discovera-
ble by chloride of iron (Woehler), citric and malic
acid (Monichini). The lemon cure in dropsy is not
only an old one, but frequently very valuable. In
Brazil they diminish by the use of lemons, the
cutaneous exhalation and increase micturition.

Many combinations deficient in nitrogen become
nitrogenous: benzoic acid, cinnamon acid, benzoic
æther, change to hippuric acid. The oil of bitter
almonds probably changes at first into benzoic acid.
Cane sugar sometimes appears as grape sugar, tannic
acid changes to gallic acid and huminous combinations. Glycine, uric acid and its salts increase the
quantity of urea.

Carbonic alkalies produce alkaline reaction in
urine and effervescence with acids. Citric, acetic,
tartaric kali and natrum are changed into carbonic
salts and are thus found in the urine: *Mascani,
Brande, Bostoch.* Kali-chlor. and natr-nitr. we get
crystallized by evaporating the urine: *Woehler,
Pereira.* Borax can be proved after destruction of
the organic parts of the urine and by addition of
sulphuric acid to the alcoholic solution by its green
color, with which the alcohol burns: *Tiedemann,
Gmelin*; Natr-sulph. is found unchanged in the urine
and its action therefore is far more extensive on the
mucous membrane of the bladder and urethra:
Grauvogl. Chlorbarium changes to sulphate of
barium: Tiedemann, Gmelin. After the use of kali
sulph. (also calcarea sulph.) an excess of sulph. acid

is found in the urine and clear traces of hydrothionic acid (Woehler.)

Woehler found Iodine after three hours. *A. Bernard* l. c., also *Heller*, Archiv 1844, p. 30. Brom *Heller* l. c., sulphur in sulphuric combination is found in the urine ; by the addition of muriatic acid a paper moistened with acetate of lead turns black by the liberated gas : *Woehler.* Petroleum can be recognised by the smell.

Gold, silver, iron, lead, tin, bismuth have been shown, ferrocyanuret of Potash after sixty minutes by *Westrumb*, on an empty stomach and with prolapsus of the inverted bladder after one minute. *Valentin*, Arsenic and antimon., after the methods of Marsh. In the urine of patients, who took for some time Natr-arsen., *Schroff* and *Schneider* found Arsen. ten days after the last dose. (Ztschr. D. W. Aerzte, Apl. 1851) Hydrargyrum was shown by Contes, Jourda, Kaiser, Oesterlen, Kletzinsky.

Some elements are not found again in the urine : Alcohol, æther, theine, caffeine, theobromine, camphor, oleum Dippelii, as they rapidly pass into new products inside of the circulation and thus become specific stimuli for brain, spinal cord and ganglia.

Smelling stuffs are very quickly excreted : oil of mustard, sabine, turpentine, almond, juniper, castoreum, valerian, asa fœt., asparagus, safran, garlic : *Bachetoni and others.*

Of coloring matter Rheum is found after 20 minutes : *Kletzinsky* in Keller's Archiv, 1852, p. 47. Senna, ibid., Madder and Indigo in 15 minutes : Safran : *Kletzinsky* l. c. Gamboge, Chelidonium :· *Huhnefeld*, Chemie und Medicin, II, 280; Campeche-wood after 25, mulberries, black cherries after 45 ; juniper sauce in 75 minutes, cassia fistula, uva ursi in 55 minutes, coccus cacti, beets, Curcuma: *Backhausen, Gruithausen et al.* Quinine as Murias, some combination of Opium, and its surrogate, the Hydrate of Chloral is probably excreted as a formic salt.

We recognize by their action on bladder and urethra : Canth., Copaiv., bals-peru, Cubebs, Petrol., Thuja, Sabina, Merc-cor.; after longer use Stannum, Lycopod.; by their action on the chemical combination of the urine and the appearance of foreign substances : Cuprum, Plumbum, Phosphor., Aurum and their preparations.

Considering the incidents of vital chemistry, we observe, that alcohol decomposes into acetic acid, Ammonia into nitric acid, whereas hydrocyanic-acid putrefies to formic-acid and urea into Carbonate of Ammonia ; i. e. according to the ideas of modern science they draw so many atoms.of water into the complex of their formula. Thus changes or decomposes animal food to animal blood, the blood progressively to tissues ; the twitching muscular fibrilla, nursed with oxygen by the arterial blood, the sensitive nervous tube and the thinking brain as well as the secreting glandular cell, they all decay at the cost of oxygen of the arterial blood into urea and all these types of decay not only run their courses without injury to life, but they rather form the very factors of life, whereas when this urea, *normally* existing by decay putrefies by the admission of innocent atoms of indifferent water $C_2N_2H_4O_2+2HO=2(CO_2N H_3)$ into Carbonate of Ammonia inside of the circulation, we witness this product of putrefaction of a nitrogenous substance, inimical to life, develop in its deleterious effects under the form of uræmia.

FREQUENCY OF THE DISEASE.

Morbus Brighti carries off a great many victims every year. *Barlow* and *Twedie* assert, that the number of healthy persons to those with diseased kidneys is as 1 to 11, *Anderson* as 1 to 6. *Bright* says, that in his times five hundred persons yearly died from renal degeneration. *Malmsten* found in 1620 patients in the Seraphin hospital of Stockholm, 69 times degenerated kidneys. *Frerich* and *Heller* increased by their physiological and chemical labor, our knowledge of this disease, so that *Kletzinsky*, 1853, and *Simon* consider the deaths by Bright's disease and by tuberculosis to be about equal.

Malmsten found among 2000 patients six times degenerated kidneys, *Rayer* thrice among 400, *Solon* only once among 500, *Finger* 46 times among 186 tuberculosis, 29 times among 88 typhus, 32 times among 46 puerperal fever, 15 times among 33 pneumonia cases.

The disease is most frequent between 20 and 40; 263 times in 491 cases, 53·5 per cent. In moist places near the sea 10 per cent. of all patients die from degeneration of the kidneys.

When the disease is frequent, many patients die from it without its being found out, as the disease begins insidiously, dropsy may be absent, and still most fatal changes take place in important organs. At the Jacob hospital at Leipzig, (1850–55,) 21 died of 37 patients, 7 of 12 of the acute form, 12 of 25 of the chronic form. ˙ Bright mentions of 24 cases six cures or ameliorations; Gregory lost 15 out of 80 cases; Andral saw two cured in 13 cases; Malmsten in 124 cases 13 cures, 43 ameliorations, 68 deaths.

Not only the frequency of the disease, but especially the death-rate and the present unsuccessful treatment oblige us, to study more this disease in order to cure more renal patients, or at least to prolong life. A dropsical patient needs six months for his rehabilitation. We hope to improve on this by a strict indication of the remedies, especially if we do not give these heroic remedies in too large doses.

We acknowledge, that among chronic cases more die from M. B., than from tuberculosis, may the kidneys have been attacked early or late, primarily or secondarily, and without counting the acute forms of uræmia, which falsely diagnosed and wrongly treated are so frequently fatal.

DURATION OF THE DISEASE.

It may only be possible in solitary cases, to fix the duration of renal disease, as it most frequently develops itself so insidiously, that the attention of the patient is not drawn towards it, until organic alterations, as in all chronic forms of gout, gonorrhœa, especially of venous origin, have made considerable progress. In acute and uræmic cases, wherefever, pain in the kidneys, vomiting, bloody urine, etc., set in, it is somewhat easier to determine the duration of the disease and its course.

The affection is not bound to any typical law, depends on variable internal and external influences, so that an insidious one may change to an acute, and one running a rapid course may become chronic, so that albuminuria as little excludes uræmia, as diabetes mellitus. The acute form may run its course in 4–6 weeks favorably or fatally, acute uræmia changes in an hour to an unfavorable issue, in a few days to recovery. The usual chronic form frequently exists for some time, and it sometimes takes years before being diagnosed, and may last years. Bright and Barlow report cases of 15 years' standing, Gregory of 30 years, and our experience is the same. Moderate albuminous forms allow moderate occupation for years. Sometimes perfect remissions set in, another time intermissions alternate with exacerbations, till a trivial cause produces a relapse. Causal circum-stances and the importance of the organic alterations in the suffering parenchymatous organs exercise the most influence on the duration.

HEREDITARY DISPOSITION.

Hereditariness of character and of morbid disposi-tions, signifies the same in the organic world, as the preservation of force in the inorganic world. Every living being is therefore the necessary result of his ancestry, and in order to understand his organisation, and the alterations in the organs, which compose it, we must give the true value to all shapes and forms of its predecessors, may they be transient or lasting, as they all give their mite by hereditariness.

We must be lenient with any new theory, as it takes three generations to give it stability, and every expert may supplement the facts, whereby he needs a long and large practice. We know that in Bright's disease we may not only acquire tubercles and other causal diseases, but that they with certainty create again a hereditary disposition, although they may pass over one generation. *Osborne* and *Prout* affirm the same of M. B., and it cannot be denied, so far as it relates to tubercles and cardiac diseases, but sufficient facts are still wanting to prove it with certainty. *Darwin* especially mentions the propagation of mental diseases, and we mention this particularly, because Darwin is since Hahnemann the only natural philosopher, who affirms the principle of similarity and treats of latent diseases. *Liebig* also acts on our law in his agricultural chemistry, but when called upon the witness stand in our behalf, he denies it—logically.

We recollect some cases, which we give as our first share to the confirmation of this opinion. We once treated the daughter, and after years her mother for uræmia. Father and daughter died from albuminous nephritis, in another case grandmother and grandchild became affected, whereas the mother suffered from hypertrophy of the left heart. Brother and sister, over seventy years old and the daughter of the former suffered from the same disease, although we cannot find in either a grave affection of the heart; once grandmother and grandchild, the daughter suffers first from jaundice, and then also the mother. The father suffers from syphilitic albuminuria, the son, 4 years old, from M. B. If syphilis, heart-diseases, especially hypertrophies are hereditary, its sequels must also be the same. Just as the disposition becomes customary in rheuma, in cardiac diseases, so also in M. B. These dispositions, which qualify the disease, can be proven in some families. A mother lost two grown-up daughters from acute tuberculosis, in after years she suffers from uræmia with vomiting and purging. A woman who died from hypertrophy of the left heart, and degeneration of the kidneys, had three sons of whom two suffer from heart-disease, whereas the third one succumbed in his youth to concentric hypertrophy from rheumatism. A woman, 62 years of age, suffered from acute uræmia, and later from intermittens, her niece, 24 years old, during typhus from M. B. A woman, 65 years old, died from hypertrophy of the left heart, to which at a late hour M. B. was joined, her son suffers from insufficiency of the mitralis; her daughter after acute rheumatism from the same disease with M. B.

From these meagre facts we deduct not only hereditariness from father to son, from mother to daughter, but also a far more general one, than in tuberculosis, from mother to son, from father to daughter, therefore also the spread of M. B. and the disposition to it so frequent, as we find it in inflammations and epidemics of different diseases. The records of life-insurance companies would throw great light on this vexed question.

PATHOLOGICAL ANATOMY.

The manner of Rokitansky still predominates, to preface the morbid phenomena with the pathological. anatomy, and Virchow does the same in his special pathology and therapy, which clearly proves, that Rokitansky stands at the head of his profession, and that physiology could not follow anatomy, as something finished, because life and death offer vital and chemical differences, which it takes time to study up. We follow the same plan and insert some remarks of our own.

The condition of the morbid kidney is different according to the causes, intensity and stage of the disease. We may accept three stages, running one into another and all three stages may be simultaneously present in chronic cases.

1. Stadium hyperæmiæ: specifically hyperæmia and cylinder, or its detritus.

2. Stadium of fatty infiltration, of degeneration; specifically the fatty degeneration of epithelia and of malpighian tufts.

3. Stadium atrophiæ, cirrhosis: specifically the atrophy of the renal substance showing itself by the small volume, by the cysts and developed pigment. Syphilitic degeneration of the kidney, comp. albuminuria.

In acute hyperæmia the kidney is enlarged to twice its normal size, its texture loosened, succulent, especially the cortical substance; at the same time full of blood, brown red, here and there infiltrated with red points, blood extravasations; on its surface starry and retiform injections, the adhesions of the albuginea are loosened. The pyramids dark brown-red, striated injected, loosened, their basal limits extinguished. The hyperæmia gradually retrocedes; but the swelling and loosening of the cortical substance increases, appearing pale-red, reddish-white, anæmic with disseminated red points and streaks from extravasation of blood, swollen over the pyramid to the thickness of 5–10 lines and largely increased in size between the pyramids, loosened, friable, nearly dissolved, fluctuating and discharging a reddish white, milky opaque fluid. In some cases it shows itself especially in the periphery granulated in larger or smaller nests, i. e. consisting of faded loose exuberant granules of the size of a poppy seed —granulations—whereas linear streaks show themselves toward the pyramids. Sometimes the granulations come out over the surface of the periphery in the form of deliquescing granulations like cauliflower excrescences. The albuginea adheres loosely, rarely only a layer of cortical substance remains adherent to it, still more rarely does bleeding happen at the periphery: the albuginea is burrowed loose by extravasations and the kidney thereby compressed; the pyramids are swelled, pale-red, on their base unravelled like a plume or sheaf. In some cases a

collateral hyperæmia develops itself with the anæmic state of the cortical substance and the pyramids
are of a dark red color. We find then usually-
striated extravasations between the tubuli, producing
after a while a rusty brown coloring of the pyramids.
The mucous membrane of the calyces and pelvis of
the kidneys is of a pink color, and in their cavities a
creamy bloody fluid. In the renal veins the blood
coagulates and makes thrombi. In the bladder a
dull, creamy, white or bloody fluid is found in small
quantities, an albuminous, bloody or pale urine.

We find sometimes with bloody effusions in the
Malpighian capsules, whose blood-vessels are pushed
to one end of the capsule and in the urinary canals
the epitheluim loosened, partly pealed off in collapsed
tubes, here and there pushed together in knotty
bunches, the urinary canals closed by them and a
finely granulated mass. After a while the peeling
off of the epithelia increases; the cells are puffed
up and become dim from a finely-granulated mass,
running together, the urinary canals therefrom uni-
formly or knottily dilated. In such a state they give
us the granulations, i. e. knots of dilated urinary
canals exuberant with epithelia pushed together.
The malpighian tufts are covered by the granular
dim epithelia, collapsed, compressed, therefore anæmic. The pyramidal tubes are also filled with a
molecular mass, coated by dim granular epithelia,
with *fibrinous cylinders*, red pigment granules are
seldom missing. The contents of the urinary organs,
in a small quantity when containing albumen and

with a deficiency of urea, show the elements of the
blood, the morbid epithelia either in solitary cells or
in membranous tubular parcels, among them also
cells of fatty granules and cylinders. Among 292
autopsies, Frerich found the first stage 20 times.

The second stage consists in *fatty, or in colloid*
(*amyloid*) metamorphosis of the epithelia. This
happens the quickest in cholera kidneys often inside of
six days, whereas in typhus it takes 2–6 months to
bring it to the same degree ; in syphilis years. In the
cortical substance of the kidney yellow points appear
solitary or grouped round a red base, either in
straight or slightly twisted lines, and the whole
kidney appears yellowish-white, pale ; the malpighian
capsules appear therein either as light or as opaque
anæmic granules, similar stripes in the pyramids—
or we find in the pale red kidney with a striated
appearance overwhelmingly a lardaceous condition of
the parenchyma with bright edges at the points of
intersection, and at the same time an increased
density. In fatty metamorphosis the epithelial cells
of both substances, but especially of the cortical one,
are changed to fatty granular cells, they separate
the cell-wall disappears and the fatty granules spread
off. The urinary canals will then be found filled
with fatty granules of different size, and blocking up
the passage, bereft of epithelium by the stagnating
secretion, dilated and collapsed. The malpighian
capsules are in the same condition, their glomeruli
shrunken. Here and there the epithelia pass into a
colloid metamorphosis, whereby the cells, filled with

a finely granulated mass, solitary or as a connected
epithelial coating, degenerate into bright, glassy, brit-
tle corpuscles, or into a connected tubular mass; a
similar state is found in the epithelia of the Bellinian
tubes, in the malpighian tufts, in the bloodvessels surrounding the urinary canals of the corticalis. In all
such speckled places the epithelia degenerated into
fatty metamorphosis. Frerichs saw this stage 139
times in 292 dissections.

In the third stage, that of *Atrophy* and shrinking,
the kidney loses in circumference, especially in the
cortical substance, according as this process takes
place more on the surface or on solitary places, the
kidney gets an equally granular tuberous surface, or
it shows large dells from loss of substance. In the
interstitia of the tuberosities the places where losses
accrue, are filled by a mass of dense connective tissue,
red in the beginning, but afterwards white, which
frequently appears as if small crystalline or opaque
vesicles were mixed in. In the cortical substance,
especially on its periphery, the connective tissue
prevails, often with interstitial pale points. During
its further course the cortical substance becomes
steadily thinner, its vascularity disappears, the greyish-
red connective tissue increases, the pyramids become
smaller, paler, covered by a thin layer of cortical
substance, to which the albuginea firmly clings.
Finally the kidney is reduced to more than half of
its volume.

The urinary canals become wasted, whereas other
parts remain in the form of vesicular formation; the

malpighian bodies fare no better. In the narrowed urinary canals varicosities appear, which separate and remain as cysts; others contain a fluid without form-elements, others are filled with a layer of cells, which are similar to the epithelia of the urinary canals, others contain a detritus, mixed with fat corpuscles, others are degenerated to dull glassy colloid bodies, perceivable by the naked eye. The malpighian bodies shrink to thick walled capsules, surrounded by concentric connective tissue, and containing the collapsed glomeruli with pigmentary and fatty granules. Frerichs found this stage 133 times in 292 dissections.

The cysts are important in rare cases, as they may become the cause of fatal issue by encroaching on or entirely suspending urinary secretion in consequence of previous M. B. They arise from dilatation and closing up of the urinary canals, from dilated malpighian capsules, from laceration of the dilated urinary canals and of the stroma, whereby the connective tissue increases in quantity all around, and many urinary canals waste away. But we must not forget, that cysts often exist without M. B., the cysts in Bright's disease are many and small, cysts as neoplasmata are large.

CHARACTER OF THE DISEASE.

The essential anatomical character of acute and chronic M. B., which, according to Hofer, is also found among domestic animals, especially horses, consists in a peeling off of the epithelium of the

urinary canals—desquamation—and their degeneration and distinguishes itself from interstitial nephritis
by the particular metamorphosis of the exudation and
of its molecular detritus. Although the usual ex-
pressions, albuminosa *Rayer*, desquamativa, *Johnson*,
parenchymatosa, *Virchow*, and croupous inflammations may be used to denote the degree of intensity,
still, and in opposition to most authors, we cannot
consider the acute disease as a croupous one, but
with *Solon, Reinhardt, de Crignis* and *Skoda*, consider
it an albuminous inflammation and for these reasons :

a. Because many a state is considered as croup,
which is far more collagene than fibrinogene; only
erethic persons expend under a rather stormy course
the fibrine, which is still present, for the exudation,
because the disease is mostly part of a general process,
which does not run its course with fibrinosis; *the
fibrine is therefore in all forms of Bright's disease dissolute, never formative;* without dissolved fibrine it
never could come to a decomposition of the urea
inside of the circulation. This dissolution causes
also the bilious appearance of acute uræmic patients
and of their urine. Neither the finely granulated
detritus, nor the formation of connective tissue, which
Johnson, Simon and Virchow deny, are of a hyperinotic nature. Even Frerichs describes the fibrine,
when it appears, as without form.

b. Because the exudation of the acute form does
not act paralysingly on the affected parts, nor are
the neighboring organs affected ex contiguitate ; the
usual inflammatory issues of hyperinotic forms are

wanting and the analysis of the blood shows no croup.

c. Because the exudation, as is the case in spasm of the nucha, is not organizable; it would be the only croupous form, which has no neoplasma as a sequel: the malpighian tufts are mostly found empty of blood, the intermediate retiform net on the contrary full of blood; the epithelium of the canals peeled off in a molecular detritus and deposited in a granular mucous intermediate fluid; finally we find the cylinder like a jelly, till at last the epithelium of the tubular substance is evacuated.

d. Because in the coarse affection of the intestinal mucous membrane in cholera—there is neither a sporadic nor an epidemic cholera without Morbus Brighti, at least no case ends fatally, where at the acme of the disease the urine does not contain large quantities of albumen and cylinders, and no typhoid follows cholera, unless we find large quantities of albumen de novo in the urine, facts forgotten by many—nobody thinks to call it a croupous affection, although the urinary canals etc. become similarly affected.

e. Because the formation of cysts, the only process which could be called a neoplasma, a dilatation of urinary canals arising from renal degeneration, belongs to the afibrinous exudations.

f. Because similar processes of other organs: chronic catarrhal pneumonia, whose exudation becomes tubercular even without a gelatinous disposition, cyrrhosis of the liver, syphilitic inflammation of the liver and especially of the kidneys, are by nobody considered[1] as croup.

On account of the want of symptoms for hyperinosis Bamberger and Buhl find a similarity between Bright's renal alteration and acute yellow atrophy of the liver, but we never find the process in the liver increased to such a degree, as in the kidney, and therefore a corresponding enlargement of the former is usually absent. An analogous alteration in the primitive fascicles of the cardiac muscles and in the parenchyma of the lungs, desquamative pneumonia, is frequently connected with either affection.

g. The fibrine here never exudates without albumen, with oxalate of lime, also a fibrinous (?) matter and sometimes with crystallised bilious fat. Finally our assertion gains affirmation:

h. From the different remedies, which have been used beneficially or wrongly. No matter what form the acute disease takes on, the exudation is never croupous, as the secondary symptoms show. We only feel astonished, that nobody has explained the whole process as a diphtheritic one, which especially in scarlatina might be tried.

ÆTIOLOGY.

Age gives no peculiar habilitation, but people from 20 to 40 years are more liable on account of their peculiar occupations, men more than women, 3 : 1, Tissot, 3 : 2, Frerichs, because they are more exposed to change of temperature, to wet and cold, according to Osborne in 48 cases 22, Malmsten in 69 cases 29, or to morning chills from exposure to the dews in the meadows—every organ, which for some length must perform a more laborious function, here on account of suppressed perspiration, is taken down with sickness—or to the use of alcoholic stimulants, among 36 diseases 10, Osborne, among 130, according to Bright, 30, according to Frerichs, 16 in 42, Malmsten 19 in 69, Bequerel, 9 in 69, in Scotland three-fourths of all cases, Christison. People working in cold damp air, going barefooted in every weather or with poor covering for their feet, as some monks, living on the coast of the Northern sea, who live poorly or are prone to excesses, are subject to this disease. Of essential influence are grief, want, syphilis, mercurial cachexia now only rarely observed, sudden suppression of cutaneous diseases (Johnson). Many, especially Peacock, consider scrofula as a predisposing cause. The Banting cure has lately also been accused of it. Among remedies, Cantharides may produce death, but never M. B. (Heller and Bouillaud observed albumen, but no tubuli in their analyses of the urine, and the former considers nephritis vera as the cause of death) but Copaiva balsam, Reinhardt, still more Turpentine, Kreasot, Petroleum, which certainly is a more important remedy than Turpentine, according to Groyer also sulphuric acid, may be the cause of Bright's disease.

Other producing causes are: all infectious diseases, miasmata and contagia, especially scarlatina, typhus, febris recurrens, diphtheritis, variola, morbilli, also pyæmia, extensive burns, ulcerations, in short all influences which greatly depress vegetative life, more rarely hooping cough; quickly appearing hydronephrosis, compression of the uterus by uterine cancer, disturbance of the abdominal venous circulation by ovarian tumors or far-advanced pregnancy, without mentioning that all due proportions to relations of pressure in the secreting parts are altered.

Direct causes of M. B. are hypertrophy of the thymus, diseases of the cardiac nerves and arthritis; the first two have so far not been mentioned, the last one only rarely.

As the hypertrophy of the thymus as a cause has never been mentioned, we may be allowed to give its changes. Its hypertrophied form is twofold: either it presents two lateral flat-round thick lobes, attaching itself on both sides to the mediastinum posticum or it forms a mass, resting more downward and like a tongue on the sac of the jugular vein. In the latter form, which after existing some time draws the kidneys in coaffection, the pathological process is the following: the tongue shaped thymus, when resting on a gonorrhœal, scrofulous or rachitic diathesis, grows in consequence of passive hyperæmia either before or after birth to the parietal part of the pericardium, whereby the left heart is so disturbed in its action, that the muscle gains in flesh, in order to perform its function. Dislocation is thus more or less produced. Whenever the pericardium attaches itself also to the serous membrane of the diaphragm, greater dislocation of the heart and of the large bloodvessels takes place, causing slow albuminous degeneration of the kidney, but more yet pulmonary stasis and capillary inflammation, because the passive stasis divides itself between lungs and kidneys, whereas in the first case, where the left heart alone becomes hypertrophied without coaffection of the diaphragm, the kidneys degenerate more quickly. The thymus may also be absorbed, but as a neoplasma may remain a cellular fibrous cord, a ligamentum thymo-cardiacum, which escapes physical examination by its thinness, but acts just as deleteri-. ous as the former thymus-hypertrophy :} by small capillary hæmorrhages in the heart, hence the pigment, dislocation and hypertrophy of the heart, thickening of the pericardium, filling of it with serous fluid, relaxation of the cardiac muscles, albuminous nephritis, coaffection of the phrenicus. When the thymus is present, the diagnosis is easy, when growing to the pericardium it becomes more difficult, the dwindling away of the gland and the presence of the ligamentous new formation can only be proven by the anamnesis and frequent auscultation of the hearts of little children. We never observed uræmia under these circumstances, but it may happen, as all the conditions for it are present.

The last mentioned forms run their course mostly to a fatal termination; they kill the seven months foetus as well as the child of eight years, suddenly, even with copious fatty deposit, which is always present on account of cardiac hypertrophy, the least in the abdomen, even when no new morbid state, as bronchitis cap., croup or cholerine is added to it; if so, so much the more certain.

The prognosis is favorable, when the organic change is still capable of retrogression by Hepar, when on account of progressing renal degeneration Aurum, Arsen. and other remedies are necessary, absolutely fatal in combinition with laryngismus stridulus, croup, pneumonia.

Among the causes of M. B. some authors mention arthritis. It produces nutritive disturbances of most diverse character : by direct organic alteration of the renal arteries, sclerosis, atheroma, softening or its combinations, also by disturbance of the venous circulation from concrements in liver, intestines, kidneys (Rayer), bladder, especially in gonorrhœic arthritis, which produces the same alterations as the gonorrhœa itself, by disturbances in the arterial circulation from insufficiency or hardness of the valves of the heart, by sclerosis etc. of the aorta, by ossification of the coronaria cordis, first known by temporary intermission of the pulse ; should it attack the basilaris, vertigo, sparks before the eyes set in according to the seat of the disease, less frequently atrophy of the brain and its sequels. When the gout is with certainty of gonorrhœic origin, the treatment is .the same as that of syphilitic nephritis.

In gouty persons with induration of the art. coron. cord, with simple dullness of the valves up to their ossification or with similar alterations in the ostia the quantity of albumen in the urine is proportionate to the vloume of the circulatory disturbances, there-

fore variable and may even disappear entirely or for
some time, according to the capability of resorption
of the infiltration.

As all organic alterations, especially of the right
heart may cause M. B. and its pregnant partial
phenomena, and as we have shown, that it may on
the part of the venous circulation emanate from the
kidneys, so we may also declare, that all immitations
of heart diseases, i. e. *affections of the nerves of the heart*,
especially hyperæsthesia, neuralgia and neuralgia
intermittens, neuroses of motility in general, may be
followed after lasting some time by uræmia up to
albuminuria, may reach in intensity the forms of the
former, but they seem to run their course in a shorter
time and are less dangerous.   Such a nervous affection
may be mistaken for incipient hypertrophy, and even
one well versed in heart-diseases may find it sometimes difficult to distinguish between them.   We
found this 4 times in 436 cases, not counting relapses.
That the nervous system possesses influence over
renal secretion and vice versa, is easily shown by the
changes during emotions and nervous diseases, as
well as by the observation, that an injury to the
fovea rhomboidalis in the fourth ventricle—not the
same place, which produces diabetes after injury, but
just above it—increases the urinary secretion and
renders the urine albuminous, but nothing certain is
yet known about the ways and mode of the actions
of nerves.   The action of nerves is probably twofold,
vasomotory, regulating the pressure in the glomeruli
and thus the filtration.   In this manner the irritated

vagus increases the circulation, so that the vein swells and the secretion increases, whereas the splanchnicus major diminishes circulation and secretion; *oxydising*, whereof the usual observations are only known. The renal venous blood is yet oxygenous, therefore crimson, probably on account of its quick through passage. According to Bernard, the irritation of the vagus renders it with increased secretion also of a lighter color, the splanchnicus darker. Compare Gilewsky.

A reproach to physiologists may be thus mentioned : have the origin-fibres of the nerves in the brain an immediate relation to the organs, on which they act or a mediate one, i. e. do they act by direct conduct or through the total mass.

General causes of desquamative nephritis, inciting the exudation, also are all mechanical and organic obstructions of the circulation, be they of arterial or venous nature, relaxation or atony of the capillaries and smaller blood-vessels, impossible without a functional disturbance, perhaps also a peculiar dyscrasia of the blood, which certainly is not any more fibrinous. It cannot be shown with any certainty from the few cases, so far observed, if thereby is also active a kind of paralysis of the blood-vessels, emanating from the spinal cord or sympathetic nerve, as in febris recurrens, in onanists, or if a direct morbid state of the nerves causes it ; in uræmia *Buhl* has shown it ; we see it most clearly in acute uræmia, in M. B. only by intimation, because the organic disturbances run a slower course in chronic cases.

Complications are :

1. All processes, which as causes precede the renal affection, or at least aid in their development, preventing the discharge of the venous blood from the kidneys, about ¼ of all cases show this cause ; abnormities of the heart and of the large blood-vessels, hypertrophy of the thymus and its adhesion to the pericardium, chronic pulmonary diseases, which encroach on the lesser circulation and thus react on the right heart ; emphysema, bronchiectasy, diseases causing deep alterations in the quality of the blood, scrofulous ulcerations, diphtheritis, tumor albus, caries and necrosis of the bones, tuberculous ulceration of the lungs, extensive burns, thrombosis of the renal veins from cancer.   2. Diseases from the same cause ; cirrhosis and fatty degeneration of the liver in consequence of drunkenness and organic heart-disease, chronic catarrh of the stomach and of the respiratory organs from the same cause, apoplexy of the lungs and of the brain in valvular diseases of the heart ; fatty degenerations of the retina, of the optic nerve, of the basilar artery.   3. Sequelæ are : inflammations of serous membranes, pneumonia, erysipelas and gangrene of the skin, especially of the feet, caused during moderate albuminuria frequently from the slightest mechanical lesion.

Which appears primarily ? the functional disturbance of the heart, the emphysema or the nephritis ; what secondarily ? remains an important question. *Traube* and *Chambers* affirm, that the hypertrophy of the heart, and the dilatation of the aortal ventricle

without valvular defect are consequences of circulatory disturbances in the kidney and of the thus
increased labor of the heart. We can only agree
under certain conditions with this close observer, as
the following facts seem to contradict it:

a. Experiments on rabbits with kali arsenicosum in
small doses produced first hypertrophy of the left
heart and then M. B.; after stopping the remedy the
renal affection disappeared first, as the examination
of the urine showed, and then that of the heart.

b. We have found in hypertrophy of the heart
as well as in valvular defects the renal function
intact for years, the urine without a trace of albumen,
without a symptom of desquamation and when the
latter are found at a late stage, they are only terminal phenomena, and prove in very many cases the
priority of the heart's affection.

c. As analogous we might adduce the hypertrophy
of the thymus, which in severe cases draws in
sympathy first the pericardium, then the left heart,
the serous coat of the diaphragm, finally the kidney,
and thus frequently kills the fœtus and nobody has
yet observed this process in a retrograde manner;
the heart must also become hypertrophic by insufficiency of the mitral valve, the degeneration of the
kidney is only a tertium. In relation to changes in
the right ventricle, they never occur except in connection with emphysema, tuberculosis, etc., without
mentioning a renal degeneration, because the course
is too slow, even if it emanated alone from the renal
veins, which Skoda disputes, because M. B. always

also would appear in any disturbance in the circulation (and it does set in when all conditions are given.)

d. In high-graded cystic degeneration of the kidneys the heart is not hypertrophic, on the contrary atrophic. It is of some importance as a curative measure, to which opinion we lean, but experiments on animals as well as observations are decisive against Traube, still there is some truth in it, as Turpentine and Copaiva seem to act in that manner and the venous degeneration from venous stagnation may sometimes emanate from the right heart, sometimes from the renal veins, especially in mechanical obstructions.

As *inconstant changes*, standing in close connection to the whole process, are known: old apoplectic foci, formation of pus in the degenerated kidney, hardly once in a hundred cases, cysts with serous fluid with little albumen, more rarely of jelly-like or fatty consistence (Johnson) and in two cases of granular deposit, containing Xanthin, nephrite goutteuse, *Rayer*, consisting mostly of uric salts, seldom of oxalic lime, renal stones probably from reflex action, when not of gouty or gonorrhœic origin, tuberculosis, diseases of the blood-vessels, atheroma of the arteria renalis, obliteration of the renal veins, of the lymphatic glands, of the hilus renalis, carcinoma.

PROGNOSIS OF THE DISEASE.

The disease may terminate in:

a. Health: especially in acute and acute urӕmic

forms, after exanthemata, cholera, typhus, localisation of recurrent fever in the lower part of the spinal cord, when the foreign elements of the urine gradually decrease, the skin becomes active and the serous effusions, if present, are absorbed. Even when all morbid phenomena pass off and albumen remains, relapses are possible. In acute forms three-fourths may remain alive, in chronic cases a perfect cure is more rare, and in complicated cases of old people, with organic destruction of different organs, we must be satisfied with prolongation of life, except when atrophy has gained a limited extension.

b. Partial recovery: when on account of destruction of a large number of urinary canals there remains a tendency to relapses or albuminuria, till the kidneys are gradually degenerated, so that they do not any more suffice for the organic household—as necessarily one part of the parenchyma with its blood-vessels becomes atrophied, when at the same time the arterial blood carries forward its quantum and thus hypertrophy sets in more or less, so that through the influence of internal or external noxae, albumen, fibrine-cylinders or carbonate of Ammonia will again appear.

c. Death: by uræmia with coma and convulsions, one-fourth of such patients, by inflammation of the serous membranes and the lungs, one-sixth; by exhaustion from vomiting and purging, by exhaustion from profuse hydropic effusions with or without gangrene, by tuberculosis, caries, asphyxia from œdema glottidis and pulmonum, or on the right side pneumonia, on the left side oedema, by hydrothorax, rarely by cerebral apoplexy.

STATISTICS.

Among the changes in other organs, which we have to consider partly as causal incidents, partly as consequences, the following deserve attention on account of the selection of the remedy.

The heart was in 436 cases 113 times hypertrophic with or without stenosis of the bicuspid valve, according to Bright 65 times in 100 cases; in children four times hypertrophic from agglutination of the thymus with the pericardium, once too small, eleven times the left valves were insufficient, once aneurisma aortæ; atheroma is found in secondary affections of the heart, as after repeated acute rheuma, in arthritis; the right heart must necessarily suffer in emphysema etc.

In 436 cases the respiratory organs were 193 times pathologically altered; according to Gregory, 23 times in 48 cases; 51 times tubercles; according to Bright in 100 cases 4, Malmsten twice in 69, Becquerel 51 times in 129, Frerichs 6 times in 42. The renal process is nearly always of older date, as generally in disturbances of the venous circulation; 76 times oedema pulmonum, 5 times oedema glottidis, especially in affection of the bicuspid, 33 times pneumonia, twice whooping-cough and pneumonia, once whooping-cough, 3 times gangrene, 9 times infarctus, 22 times vesicular oedema, 3 times emphysema, once exquisite gonorrhœic perichondritis, once bronchitis.

Inflammation of serous membranes set in 43 times in the pleura, according to Bright 26 times in 100 patients, once at the diaphragm, 39 times at the peritoneum, 13 times at the pericardium, 3 times at the endocardium.

In the stomach there was 21 times chronic catarrh in drunkards, 4 times perforating ulcer, 6 times carcinoma, 3 times black softening of the stomach.

Among 436 cases the liver was 48 times diseased, 28 times cirrhotic, 19 times fatty degenerated; Andral found it 23 times diseased in 65 patients, according to Bright 60 times in a hundred; at any rate more frequently after drinking spirits, than after beer or wine. Hepatic and renal diseases seem to have the same causes.

Splenetic swellings are present, when the disease develops itself in the course of typhus, or when intermittens appears as a symptom in patients, suffering from fatty heart, but it may also be caused by qualitative changes of the blood, according to Bright 30 : 292.

Hyperæmia of the spermatic veins in pregnant and lying-in women 9 times.

Twice pancreatic disease, once psoitis, once intestinal calculi, twice renal calculi, once suppuration of the salivary glands, once suppuration of the left inguinal gland, once of the prostata, 9 times osseous diseases.

Cerebral apoplexy, ten times in 292 cases, has its cause in diseases of the heart and of the large blood-vessels, and thus we find degenerated kidneys in paralysed persons.

Of 120 cases, 13 were affected with uræmic amblyopia and amaurosis, (amaurose albuminurique, Landousi), 10 with difficulty of hearing. The former may be caused by degeneration of the retina and bloody effusion in it. We hold fast to the nutritive disturbance, and consider the organic alterations accidental. Uræmia has the same effect on the optic nerves as on other nerves, produces irritation, hyperæsthesia or paralysis, anæsthesia, or as in the kidneys fatty degeneration of the retina takes place, as also observed by Zenker. The state of the retina may be compared in such cases to hæmorrhagia punctata. Such visual disturbances are also met in diabetes. Lichtenstein wrote a splendid dissertation about it (Comp. Virchow's Archiv, 10, 170). That heart-diseases dispose to amaurosis, was known long ago, Virchow reduces the whole process to embolism.

The movable kidney for itself produces not M. B., but the combination with tuberculosis, hepatic diseases will do it. Rollet found in 22 cases of movable kidney twice M. B., in consequence of pathological changes already mentioned. We would finally mention, that causes and consequences are frequently found together, pneumonia on the right side and œdema on the left, right hydrothorax, left œdema, coxalgia and pleuritis.

The disease runs its course without dropsy, as 1: 7, according to the autopsies as 1: 4. Gregory found dropsy 22 times in 80 cases, Christison 4 times in 31, Frerichs 29 in 41.

According to clinical observations in 150 cases of M. B., there was cerebral œdema 4, apoplexy 2, hydrophtalmos 1, diseases of the retina and of the optic nerves 6, softening of the thalamus opticus 1, retinitis 1, amblyopia from fatty degeneration of a part of the optic nerve 1, amaurosis 2, endophtalmia 1, carditis 2, left cardiac hypertrophy 13, insufficiency of the valves of the right heart 1, right side dilated 1, fatty degeneration 1, eccentric hypertrophy of the heart 1, adhesion of the valves of the right heart 1, bronchitis 2, pneumonia with insufficiency of the mitralis 1, pneumonia 3, emphysema with insufficiency of the mitralis 1, emphysema 17, œdema pulmonum 9, phthisis pulmonalis 11, pleuritis 17, peritonitis 5, endometritis 1, hepatic cysts 1, hepatic cancer and phthisis pulmonalis 1 ; of infectious diseases morbilli 1, variola 1, typhus 2 ; caries 6 times.

Of 491 deaths from degeneration of the kidneys, there were 10: 1–10 years old, 44: 10–20, 263 : 20–40, 146 : 40–60, 28 : 60–80.

DIAGNOSIS.

The diagnosis of M. B. offers no difficulties, although the disease is often overlooked for a long time, and treated in a wrong manner.

Characteristic phenomena are: the quality of the urine. a. The sediment consists of *epithelia* of the *tubulae Bellini* and of the *Malpighian tufts*, exquisite globuli, which strung together like sausages give us Henle's cylinders, or fatty globules; fatty infiltrated epithelia or crystals of uric acid, especially of triple phosphates or blood corpuscles, pus cells. b. The quantity of albumen with or without simultaneously present renal anasarca or ascites. Some consider albuminuria as a characteristic symptom of M. B.; this is wrong, renal elements are essential and necessary for it. In relation to the well-known reaction of Nitric acid on albumen we would remark, that the moderately-diluted acid should be added in a white vial, to a third of the urine in an oblique angle by pronation of the vial, in order that it may act from below upwards; that the opaque dullness may be also produced by a surplus of phosphoric salts of lime, and, by the use of resinous remedies, as Copaiva, is well known, these salts dissolve in acetic acid, and the presence of resin and balsamic articles may be known by the smell as well as by the fact that they make no deposit. By examining with a microscope the precipitate, made with the Nitric acid, of urine impregnated with the active principle of Cubebs or Copaiva, we find it consisting of small oily drops, easily soluble in ether. In boiling it we would remark, that alkaline and neutral urine drops the albumen only with difficulty or not at all, as the albuminates of alkalies, like cheesy matter, are soluble in boiling water, and it is therefore necessary to render it acid by acetic acid.

c. The salts and the urea are diminished, its specific weight less, in cases far progressed 1006–1012, the blood contains therefore more salts and less albumen.

d. The color is different, in acute cases like water, in which meat was soaked, containing many blood corpuscles or pale with many small emulsive globules or as in icteric persons, in chronic cases mostly pale, brown in unfavorable cases, inclining to analbuminuria. Albuminous urine of chronic patients foams easily, especially when carrying or shaking it.

2. Pain in the region of the kidney, either spontaneous or after pressure ;

3. Hydrops, which may be missing, when the urine contains much albumen and only a few renal elements ; it has no decided point of beginning ; whereas in cardiac diseases it begins constantly with œdema pedum, in granulated liver with ascites, it may begin in Hydrops Brighti at the most different points, passes off at one point and appears at another. It frequently sets in, as in scarlatina, with œdema of the face and of the joints.

4. Catarrhs, inflammations of the lungs, of the serous membranes are not constant phenomena.

5. Anomalies in the vegetative and animal functions are : gastric troubles, dyspepsia, vomiting, diarrhœa, the most frequent cause of it the deposition of urea on the mucous membrane of the stomach in the form of Carbonate of Ammonia, found also in animals after tying the kidneys, when immediately severe vomiting set in and the vomited matter contained Ammonia.

Other functional disturbances in consequence of

the disease, as pseudorheumatismus, give only hints
to the selection of the remedy.

The diagnosis is therefore easy, but the secondary
symptoms, as vomiting, spasms, palpitation, fatty degeneration of different organs, appear sometimes
with such force, that they overshadow the real seat
of the disease, as the renal region is in most cases
painless and only shows some sensitiveness to pressure, or the urine by simple looking at it may fail to
show any phenomena.

Diseases, which on account of their similarity
might be mistaken for degenerated kidneys, are:
nephritis with its many pains, only in the circumference of the inflammation small quantities of albumen may enter the urinary tract, but never cylinders.
Renal hæmorrhage, tuberculosis, hydronephrosis,
echinococcus, diaphragmitis in its crura. Different
gastric troubles could only be supposed, as long as
the urine is neglected to be examined.

PROGNOSIS.

A perfect cure is only possible in acute cases without any complications, for urinary canals, filled for
too long a time with non-organisable exudation, become atrophied and never regain their functional
power. Solitary cicatrized places may be borne
without detriment to the organismus. The cause of
the disease plays an important part: when the action
is ephemeral, as in acute exanthemata, typhus, febris
recurrens, the course of the disease will also be more
favorable than in incurable organic alterations, like

tuberculosis. The secondary symptoms, hydrops, may be treated successfully till the kidneys become degenerated and the blood too much changed in its composition. With the decrease of dropsy the danger of uræmia may increase. Uræmia is of evil omen in the last stage of the disease, in cholera without the algid state, as we witness it towards the end of epidemics. By comparing the disgusting skeleton of a gonorrhœic lung with syphilitic nephritis, we may consider that the latter runs a slow course.

The prognosis is more favorable, when M. B. sets in during the course of an inflammation, than when it was originally present.

Vomiting passes off with the diminution of the violent congestion of the kidneys, more slowly in drunkards, in diseases of the heart and of the diaphragm. Uræmic vomiting ceases with increasing urinary secretion. Catarrhs are stubborn in hydræmia and disturbances of the lesser circulation.

Disappearance of Carbonate of Ammonia and instead of it albumen, decrease of albumen with increase of specific weight of the urine is favorable; unfavorable the disappearance of the albumen with scanty secretion of urine.

Complications, as inflammations, render the disease more dangerous.

Acute intense M. B. may kill in the stage of hyperæmia or in the consequent stage of anæmia with symptoms of uræmia from retention of urea with slight infiltration of the subcutaneous connective tissue. In the second stage the disease becomes fatal after a while with the symptoms of uræmia and hydrops and other accidents, in cachectic persons from exhaustion. In the third stage the original causes produce the fatal issue, as cardiac diseases from dropsy, inflammations with consequent exhaustion, hydrops with mortification of the skin and of the cellular tissue.

Formerly it was thought, that two-thirds of all acute cases and one-eighth of the chronic ones may recover.

SYMPTOMS AND COURSE.

We distinguish an acute and a chronic form, of which the former frequently, according to its more rapid or slower cause, the latter rarely terminates in recovery.

The acute form manifests itself sometimes by prodroma : slight affections of the crura diaphragmatica, of the diaphragm, of the stomach, dyspepsia, chills, heat, full hard pulse, malaise, nausea, dry hot skin, sometimes and even more frequently such manifestations are wanting and only a severe pain in the renal region sets in, especially after stooping or by pressure ; but even this may be absent and the patient only recognizes his disease by its consecutive symptoms, a frequent inclination to urinate (explained by Frerichs by a morbid irritability of the nerves of the bladder, a hyperæsthesia and hence hypertrophy of the muscles of the bladder) by scanty discharge of the urine, which looks red, bloody, more rarely yellow, but muddy, is mostly of acid reaction and greater specific weight, contains less urea and chlorides, shows in boiling and especially by addition of nitric acid, albumen, less at the start, but more during the progress of the disease, deposits in the vessel a red sediment, consisting of blood globules, epithelium and fibrinous cylinders, according to Johnson sometimes also of coagula, very similar to wax, the waxy cylinders. The renal region shows extension of dullness by percussion. The phenomena, caused by reduced excretion of water, quickly follow, as loss of albumen, fibrine and blood-corpuscles; when the intestines, cutis and lungs fail to discharge more water than normally, the blood becomes more watery, diminished nutrition of the body follows, the capillaries lose their resistance and exudate, œdema will be present. This may set in on all possible places, as partial, but usually appears at first on the feet or on the face, or on the labia pudendi or the tunica vagin. prop. testis, and our duty is to immediately examine the urine. It spreads rapidly over the extremities, the abdomen, over the whole body and frequently migrates from one place to another. Simultaneously dropsy of the cavities sets in, of the pleura, of the pericardium, of the cerebral ventricles, especially ascites, but the latter does not always stand in direct proportion to that of the skin, so that both are not always equally severe. With their appearance the inflammatory symptoms decrease more and more. But where intestines, skin and bronchia compensate for the activity of the kidneys, neither œdema nor dropsy will arise, but

4

instead disturbed gastric digestion, vomiting, loss of appetite, thirst and diarrhœa or bronchoblennorrhœa, cough, dyspnœa, asthma, even emphysema or morbid states of the skin, itching eruptions. Where these excretions do not suffice, and that is frequently the case, disturbances in nervous action set in in the brain and peripheric nerves, as : vértigo, convulsions, colic, palpitation, gastralgia, vomiting, etc. In such cases the acute form already passes over into the chronic one. All dropsical symptoms disappear rapidly, as soon as perspiration sets in with a decrease of fever, of albumen and blood in the urine, with copious micturition and return of urea in the urine, and recovery takes place in a few days. But the entire process is not always fully extinguished, there remain mostly disturbances in the renal functions, albumen in the urine, and the slightest cause produces a relapse of the M. B. In other cases the patients die, either by complication of peritonitis, pleuritis, meningitis and other inflammations, or by retention of urine in the blood, causing headache, sopor, coma, convulsions, etc. ; the acute, uræmic intoxication.

The chronic form either develops itself from the acute, or it appears gradually and quietly. Pains in the renal region, which in the former frequently are of great intensity and radiating to the testicles and to the diaphragm, are here entirely missing, or are only felt after deep and strong pressure. The attention of the patient is only led to his disease by the frequent, especially *nocturnal* inclination to urinate or by the *thirst*, lasting for months and not quenched.

by drinking. Though only a small quantity at a time of watery, pale, acid or neutral urine of low specific gravity is passed, still it amounts to a large quantity on account of the frequent discharge. The slight sediment always shows under the microscope the pathological alterations of the kidneys, epithelial cells, cylinders smooth or with an epithelial covering or containing fatty particles, according to the stage, exudation casts, but no blood-corpuscles; at every new relapse, symptoms of the acute form. Albumen is shown in larger quantities at the beginning of the disease and during exacerbations, in less quantities when the symptoms decrease. The daily loss of albumen amounts to 5–15 grammes, rarely more, specific gravity between 1015–1030, in more advanced stages 1004–1012. The peculiar odor of urine is entirely gone and reminds one of serum or poor beef-tea.

The face of the patient in consequence of the profound alteration of the blood-crasis becomes pale, pasty, stupid, his mind weighed down, the skin dry and cool, dropsical swellings set in, at first on the eyelids, hands, feet, scrotum, then over the whole body, and in the cavities of the chest and abdomen.

The skin, thus too much stretched, becomes inflamed and gangrenous, alleviating the other states and restraining the uræmia. Or disturbances and morbid affections of the intestinal tract, of the respiratory organs, according to Christison also neuralgiæ of the extremities or chronic articular rheumatismus, or cerebral and spinal manifestations appear, all of them sooner or later leading to a fatal issue. But death

may also follow from the complications of M. B.
already mentioned, may they precede it, or be its
cause, or become added to it. Restoration to health
is the exception, and then all manifestations gradually
decline, in most cases the gradual atrophy of the
renal substance causes a tedious ailment, having its
paroxysms and apyrexia, raising the hope of returning health in the patient, but carrying him steadily
forward to the grave. The disease increases and decreases, remains in statu quo for a shorter or longer
time, the dropsy and the albumen disappear, but the
kidney steadily shrinks, or a relapse occurs, another
till now healthy part is attacked, till finally the whole
kidney is atrophic and unable to perform its function
and the patient succumbs, frequently after years,
mostly under manifestations of uræmic intoxication.
He feels lazy and sleepy, gets a stupid cold face,
complains of terrible headache; his mind is obscured,
sopor, interrupted by mild deliria occurs, respiration
becomes stertorous, tremor of the hands, convulsions
of the face, then of the whole muscular system set in,
finally death. Or all prodroma are wanting, symptoms of cerebral depression or cerebral irritation
appear suddenly. In the first case, severe headache,
vertigo, nausea, vomiting, sopor, with pale face, injected conjunctiva, contracted pupil, circumscribed
redness of the cheeks, hard full even pulse, quick
rattling breathing; in the second, convulsions over
the whole muscular system, similar to eclampsia;
the senses also become affected: amblyopia, amaurosis, loss of hearing, of taste and of smell appear, also

digestive troubles, nausea and diarrhœa or only vomiting of green masses; more rarely a torpid fever in the vascular system. The excretions, in the beginning acid, then urinous, containing larger quantities of urea.

We would finally remark, that the different forms, suddenly or slowly, may pass one into another, as e. g. Albuminuria into uræmia, and vice versa.

DIET.

In relation to diet everything has to be avoided, which acts medicinally on the kidneys. Champagne, Moselle, parsley, onions, asparagus, etc. etc. Diuretic remedies may, but sometimes fail to ameliorate the serous transudations in the skin or in the cavities produced by the disturbances in the circulation and in the quality of the blood, but they will aggravate the state of the blood; when e. g. in heart disease— Osborne—œdema of the feet is removed by the use of parsley, Juniper, Squills, the patient dies sooner, because through the artificially congestive state the Bellinian tubes and the Malpighian tufts perish, fatty degeneration increases and atrophy must follow.

Milk-cures are recommended; in connection with diaphoretics and hot baths they cannot be considered as such. Miscat summa profundis.

Warm baths of 32° R. followed by sweating in bed, may reduce immense dropsies: Osborne, Niemeyer. In acute cases let the diet be most simple; in chronic cases, animal food, red wines or beer may be recommended, if the stomach is not troubled by Carbonate of Ammonia.

PROPHYLAXIS.

Ut vivas igitur, vigila.

Hor. Sat. II. 3, 152.

The prevention of disease, a work of utmost importance to all physicians is ever, when cognizance is taken of all ætiological influences, connected with unsurmountable difficulties, they being unable to prescribe to laborers the choice of their occupation, to regulate time and place, or to give them healthy dwellings, healthy food and clothing, or to prevent misery and want, or to proscribe injurious beverages qualitatively or quantitatively; in fact sanitary measures which we wish to carry out, are too often the stumbling block, which we are unable to remove. The lower strata of society, which pass their days in sorrow and hard labor, where poverty and gin go hand in hand, do not listen to the admonition of a physician. In 436 cases we met three, where the patients accommodated themselves in such a degree to their disease, that they asked for aid only three days before their death from general dropsy. Our education is still greatly at fault, which teaches more about Egypt, than of the human body. We can only advice and do our best. He who values his life and the time of its productiveness, may keep many an evil hour away, if taught how to prevent evil consequences.

In acute exanthemata, diphtheria, typhus, patients and reconvalescents must be warned against atmospheric changes.

Patients of the higher classes usually are more careful of their health, and are better able to carry out our admonitions. Here we may even succeed in moderating hereditary tendencies and morbid dispositions, among which we also count M. B. and its causes. Let us give our full attention to gonorrhœas and condylomata of young people, and let us not surfeit them with balsamic remedies. Astringent injections are also injurious. The former destroy the kidneys by albuminuria, the latter produce metastasis.

THERAPIA.

Nil audire velim, nil discere, quod levet ægrum.

Hor. Ep. I. 8. 8.

In science the time of blind belief has passed away, and to knowledge is the tendency of the world : every subservient tendency, not emanating from a principle, as at the time of Æneas Sylvius, is banished. When we know the first desideratum of a diagnosis, the pathological changes in the different organs and the symptoms peculiar to the diseased person, the more important one follows : which remedies will remove the present organic disturbances in that patient, what is the diagnosis of the remedy. Nobody will be cured by the diagnosis of the disease, if we do not know how to find a remedy for it. A certain patient (not a certain disease) needs a certain remedy. We steadily oppose such an idea, as if a remedy must be given to make sick, not to restore health, as it is so often the case in the old school, when they intend to act with full force. The curative indica-

tions change also with the stage of the disease, with
ætiological influences and with the consequences,
by which they act on the blood-crasis of different
individuals.

It will not suffice, to name specific remedies for
the disease, but we must give a differential diagnosis,
which the old school totally ignores, in other words,
only an individual specific remedy can be of use and
our treatment is in every solitary case a discovery.
There are no organ remedies. The catarrh of Nux,
the fibrinous exudation of Cantharides, recommended
by Wells and Rayer in M. B., the uric fermentation
of Lycopodium, the sugar from Plumbum, the pus
from Sulphur are in certain cases not of sufficient
importance, because the cylinders, the emulsive
globules, the epithelia, the exudation-casts are not
found in the provings on healthy persons, even when
albumen shows itself in the urine, as in all remedies,
which cause arterial hyperæmia or venous stasis of
the kidneys. We find in different remedial and
morbid actions, that the same phenomena arise from
different causes, as Arsen., Phosphor., Cuprum, and
we therefore say : Morbus Brighti = Albuminuria +
renal elements, as Urea + 1 per cent. water = Carbonate of Ammonia or Uræmia.

According to our ideas of albuminous nephritis,
all hyperinotic remedies like Aconite, are dismissed,
because the present fever is not a fibrinous one.
Skoda and Iaksch justly deny any successful results
to abstraction of blood or to cold.

Every remedy specific to the disease, may be

indicated under certain conditions, but a universal specific exists as little as in intermittent or typhus. Let us therefore try to give the differential diagnosis of the remedies. The most important are: Turpentine, Arsenic, Phosphor., Cuprum, Aurum and their different combinations, among the plants perhaps Belladonna, Bryonia and Colchicum, in a minor degree Digitalis and Dulcamara, too much neglected in spinal inflammations.

Oil of Turpentine (according to Kidd) has: scanty secretions of urine, dark, sometimes bloody urine, coagulating by heat and Nitric acid; under the microscope cylindrical coagula, renal elements, oxalate of lime,* large renal anasarca, irritability and debility of the intestinal tract, anorexia, copious mucous expectoration, physiognomy sallow, suffering, sunken. Every organic alteration of the heart and large blood-vessels, so frequently present among the inhabitants of the European continent, renders turpentine useless, it may be possible to be of more benefit in England on account of climacteric influences. Workmen in India-rubber factories, where turpentine is largely used, die from M. B. The same may be said from Balsam. Copaiva, if given in large doses for curative purposes, only it acts less intensively, and our obser-vations are restricted to gonorrhœic patients and therefore are only of comparative value. There are

---

* *Home* already knew the inflammation of the urinary organs by Turpentine and *Johnson* drew coagula of oxalate crystals, evacuated in consequence of the application of this oil.

4*

some patients, where Albuminuria and Anasarca showed themselves. In one case the balsam produced at first a lasting intestinal catarrh, affected then the left heart with great asthma, then the kidneys, and the patient only died after a lapse of years with uræmic symptoms. Hydropathic treatment under Priesnitz gave no beneficial results. Such a case would support the views of *Traube*, but more anon under Phosphorus.

Statistics prove that one-fourth of all persons, suffering from renal degeneration, have to ascribe its origin to hypertrophy of the left heart, whereas the right heart, either directly through the lesser circulation or indirectly through the vena cava ascendens is less frequently concerned in it. Hence follows that we have to look for remedies, which in their physiological effects not only affect the kidneys in a similar manner, but which also disturb the activity of the right or left heart; Arsen. is the representative of nutritive disturbances in the left heart, Phosphorus of the same in the right heart with simultaneous or consequent alteration of the renal substance.

Arsenical preparations, especially kali arsenicosum, constantly differ from all other remedies, in that they produce only M. B., after the left heart becomes hypertrophied, the aorta expanded, i. e., secondarily. We find this to such a degree, that after omitting the remedy, e. g. in rabbits, the affection of the kidney retires, whereas the cardiac hypertrophy continues in a lighter degree and also disappears after omitting the remedy. Although the kidneys, as also observed by Orfila, are only secondarily affected by arsenic, the intestinal tract is only a tertiary focus of localization, except where too large a dose produces chemical action, all of which we find in a far higher degree with arsenicum in regard to the kidneys, then with turpentine and copaiva, which have not the primary action on the cardiac muscle and the intestinal muscular coat. Arsenic urine shows all the changes of Morbus Brighti, from albumen of only opaque dullness to gelatinous coagulation of the urine by nitric acid, from simple epithelium and its fatty degeneration to atrophy of the Bellinian tubes, of the Malpighian tufts and of the capsule of Muller; it produces a hyperinotic blood-crasis with tendency to hydræmia, just like M. B., so that all the objective phenomena, as they are found in the experiments made by Quaglio, justify its application, where the left heart is principally affected.

Arsenic causes also disturbances, as from abuse of wine or spirits, symptoms as from the effects of moist cold, paralysis of the lower third of the spinal cord, uræmic spasms in the sensory nerves, whereas cuprum attacks the motory ones, severe paroxysms of suffocation from emphysema, intermittent neuralgia, watery exudations and transudations, as from organic alterations of the left heart and of the large blood-vessels. Vomiting from uræmia, nephritic colic (therefore also applicable in concrements, which change in such a manner the substance of the kidney and whereby patients frequently complain of spasms in the chest and stomach) urine of all sorts, even bloody, total suppression of urine, but not for so long a time as Merc. cor.

General physiological indications for Arsenic are: paroxysms of anguish at night, forcing him out of bed, stitches in the renal region when breathing or sneezing, vomiting of brown matter with severe colicky pains, vomiting after all food, pressure in the pit of the stomach, burning pain in the stomach and pit of stomach, difficult micturition, strangury, swelling of the sexual organs, ascites ; *special indications:* in the head : delirium from time to time returning, the senses are in morbid activity ; stupefaction of the head with vertigo. Excessive headaches; periodical headache. Heaviness and dullness of the head, so that he cannot rise up, and must lie down. Severe hammering pains over the whole head; especially in the forehead, with nausea when trying to rise up in bed. Swelling of the head and face, of the eyes and neck. The chest symptoms 681–760 are clearly of a threefold nature. a. From circulatory disturbances, to which also belong the serous exudations and transudations. b. From asthma ex cardiac disease, alterations in the arteries, emphysema. c. From albuminous nephritis.

There are not many heart symptoms, but they are distinct : all sorts of palpitations and most different pulses : intermittent, as in calcification of the coronaria cordis, rapid, feeble, tense, slow.

Gastric phenomena 435–503 show : vomiting of yellow-green mucus and water with very bitter taste in the mouth, as observed in uræmia, vomiting of mucus and green bile. When the vomiting decreases frequent and extremely watery diarrhœa sets in. During the vomiting severe internal heat and thirst. In the stomach itself all sorts of troubles.

In relation to the urine its primary effect is suppression of urine, diminished secretion of urine. The recent examinations of the urine by Quaglio clearly demonstrated the quality of the Arsenical urine.

The antipode of the versatile Arsenicum, decidedly opposite in the producing causes, is *Phosphorus**, which

---

* How important the doctrine is of the relationship of remedies, of the lateral action (toward the right or left) here in relation to the two sides of the heart, the following cases show: a young lady, 22 years old, had suffered probably already during her second pregnancy in consequence of an affection of the spermatical veins from M. B. After a natural confinement severe uterine hæmorrhage (frequently seen in patients suffering from renal diseases) set in, and on the 14th day eclampsia. After two days more the two physicians, who treated her, declared her lost, a third one remarked that only a miracle could save her, about midnight they expected her death. At 10 P. M. we found the patient paralysed on the right side, convulsed on the left side, right atrophy, left œdema of the brain, unconscious even in the intervals, could not move mouth, tongue or fauces. Position on the back, slight rattling, hypertrophy of left heart. Suppression of urine. Stram. struck us favorably, but the urine drawn with the catheter showed Ammonia, renal epithelia and some albumen. Cuprum for two days, followed by Arsenicum removed in very short time all her troubles, restored the muscular mobility, only the right hand remained a little awkward, but she can sew and knit.

In another case three physicians considered a man of 62

Hahnemann does not find indicated in great debility and want of vitality. The renal symptoms 1009–1061 show a deep disturbance of this organ, with which the cardiac symptoms 1270–78 are in very close connection. These symptoms may be thus explained.

1. *Sorge* remarks: Phosphor-urine contained several times large quantities of epithelia, pus and mucous corpuscles, in six cases albumen, in two exudation-cylinders and once blood-corpuscles.

2. *Nitsche* gives a post-mortem of a man, poisoned by Phosphorus: Kidneys degenerated as in M. B., the cortical substance slightly granulated, the corpora Malpighii and Rete strongly injected, in the urinary canals exudation-casts. With it the first stages of pneumonia. The urine showed during life albumen and exudation-cylinders, a higher specific gravity,

----

years, moribund. He formerly suffered from gout, has now cerebral œdema, therefore apathy, is only conscious for a little while, replies incorrectly or not at all to questions, suffers from dilatation of the right heart caused by atheroma of the pulmonary arteries, from fatty liver. His urine shows moderately albumen and renal elements, no ammonia. Phosphorus soon brought amelioration, an arthritic attack retarded a journey to the country, but the man is again able to perform his work.

There can be no better proof of the excellence of our therapeutic measures, than when patients given up as lost by the old school, are restored to health by Homœopathy and to the performance of their daily labors. Even when life is only prolonged for a decennium, the result is favorable to us in comparison with other methods of cure.

an increase of the sulphuric and phosphoric salts, a decrease of the chlorides.

3. A woman took some phosphor. in her soup : nausea, vomiting, pressure in the chest, dyspnœa, swelling and sensitiveness of the mammæ, albumen in the urine and some renal elements. Phosphor. must have caused an uræmic state, in case the vomiting emanated from the renal affection, which, though probable, cannot be proved by one case. I. O. Muller failed to examine the urine in the case of poisoning, which he treated, but Flachsland saw nephritis from this remedy.

The following *general indications* can be given for Phosphorus, the chief representative of albuminous exudation in the substance of the lungs (Wurmb, Liedbeck) : the presence of tuberculosis, also especially of diseases of the right heart or of the pulmonary artery or of both, distinguishing themselves principally by passive venous stagnations in the kidneys. The chief physiological reason for the application of Phosphorus is therefore diametrically opposed to that of Arsenicum, as they bear a proportion as right and left : Arsenicum affecting the left heart, Phosphor. the right one, or in other words, the former causes arterial stagnation, the latter venous stagnation with or without disturbance of the lesser circulation. The granulated kidney in typhus may therefore indicate Arsen. under certain conditions ; with much rattling murmurs in the bronchi, with coagulation in the pulmonary artery, in the right heart, with hypostasis of the lungs, with torpid state : Phosphorus, also in suppuration of bones. When typhus is epidemic and M. B. is a characteristic symptom, Acid-phosph. is preferable, as in poisoning by carbonic-acid during epidemic croup (Kammerer) i. e., in diphtheritis, in epidemic pneumonia. It is well known, that painless exhausting diarrhœas are characteristic of phosphoric acid. It diminishes the dropsy by liberating the capillaries from the nutritive disturbances of a venous nature. It is hardly necessary to show the great value of Phosphorus as a vascular remedy.

The gross nutritive disturbances in the brain, etc., found in acute and uræmic diseases, agree with the symptoms of Phosphor., observed in provings 80, 90, 91, 93, 95, 96, 97, 99, 103–7, 116, 117, 136, 145, 149, 153–6, 162–6, 170.

We want to draw your attention particularly to these phenomena, because in eclampsia the question arises, Phosphor. or Arsenic. The solution is simple : Phosphor. in symptoms of cerebral atrophy, Arsen. in œdema cerebri.

The hundred symptoms, recorded in the Materia Medica on the action of Phosph. on the eye, clearly prove, that not only the uræmic affection of the optic nerves, but also the fatty degeneration of single parts of the retina, or of solitary nervous fibrillæ belong to our remedy, especially when combined with other phenomena, or where we can demonstrate Atheroma of the arteries or of the muscles of the heart. In the latter case we found also intermittent fever, for which Quinine is of no benefit, but which will be cured by Phosph.

Other reasons lead us to the application of *Phosphoric acid.* The disease is more procrastinating than chronic, with the character of excessive torpidity; the crasis is, so to say, not hydræmic, not aglobulous, but melanotic, similar to scurvy and typhus stupidus, as they may arise in relaxed, thin-walled and expanded hearts and in drunkards, where we find far more frequently atheromatous arteries and petechiæ, than ossifications and indurations. The beginning of such renal degeneration is very lingering, concealed, mistaken for everything else, frequently simulating typhoid fevers, but considering the utmost indifference towards all and everything, the dull behavior even with delirium, and the apathy to eating and drinking lasting for weeks; a strict examination of the urine, the frequent vomiting and the nausea, the rare somnolency, the loose and bleeding gums, the sensitiveness of the renal region, though only slight in many cases, with the absence of the splenetic tumor and painfulness in the cœcum, will lead us to diagnose a parenchymatous degeneration of the renal tissue (nephritis). The urine contains phosphate of lime, fatty globules, fibrinous and epithelial detritus, rarely carbonate of Ammonia, and never much albumen. The bowels are always very inactive, and we have none or light-yellow diarrhœa (as in the so-called Cholera-typhoid); no fever, no heat, no reactionary symptoms, sallow cool skin, cool perspiration, urine like whey, then fawn-colored, finally like lemonade with larger quantities of albumen and appetite returns. Œdema and hydrops are absent,

but hypostatic pneumonia may be present. Prognosis rarely hopeless for this form of the disease—429,
431, 432 hint to M. B.

We have no special indication for *Sulphur*, the
phlegmatic brother of Phosphorus; it is a powerful
absorbent, but there are no plastic exudations in
granulated kidney, and for the dilatation of the
canals in form of cysts or for cysts generally, if we
could diagnose them, Calcarea would be more in its
place. *Kafka* recommends Hepar, especially in M.
B. after scarlatina.

Calcarea phosphorica and arsenicosa deserve consideration under certain conditions, although the
animal lime-earth, though producing fatty degeneration, acts like a cord on Clisson's capsule, devastates
the hepatic cells, but does not act on the renal parts
disturbed by M. B., still it gives us disturbances
from catching cold and from working in water, pains
in the urinary organs after getting the feet wet, all of
which are also found under M. B. In combination
with acids the action of the lime-earth not only
becomes modified, as *Hering* proved in Calc-ars., but
peculiar. We use Calc-phosph. in Scrofulosis, osseous
diseases, tuberculosis, Calc-ars. in girls with ulcers of
the stomach, defective menstruation, in Hypertrophy
of the pancreas, in pregnancy with albuminuria, in
simultaneous embolism and after M. B. has passed
off. No physician should make at this day such a
mistake as to prescribe ferrum in degeneration of the
kidneys, where he ought to give the life-prolonging
Calcarea and its preparations.

By comparing the actions of Arsenic and Copper, we find a great superficial similarity, but the symptoms arise from different causes. In order to prove them physiologically and chemically for renal degeneration, we instituted provings on animals with Arsen., Aurum and *Cuprum,** and arrived with Cuprum aceticum to the result, that it attacks more slowly than Arsen. the left cardiac muscle, and this more directly through the motory cardiac nerves than by clear hypertrophy, which never reaches a high degree on account of the debilitation of the energy of the heart; neither does it attack so acutely as Arsen., but changes more durably, so that it will be more difficult to bring them back to their former state, the internal coat and muscular coat of the arteries, nearly simultaneously the arterial and venous circulation and there mostly that of the liver and kidneyst—hus the poverty of phenomena partly on account of the slow lesion with simultaneous wasting of the muscles, partly on account of want of reaction in those organs during gradual nutritive disturbances, for all these organs, especially the liver, give very few symptoms under such conditions. Cuprum, when not acting anhydrosic, causes therefore ascites dependent on cirrhosis of the liver, where

---

* *Kletzinsky* once remarked : that remedy, which produces in the urine albumen plus renal elements, must be one of the best remedies in Cholera. We must only add to that declaration, " without previously altering the blood-carrying organs," or else Arsen., Phosph., Aurum, etc., had to be counted in ; the remedy is Cuprum.

copper can also be chemically demonstrated. (We know of no remedy which shows better indications in syphilitic hepatitis, than Cuprum, all other remedies, even Mercur. and Iodine, give only negative results.)

Cuprum in small doses also produces far quicker than Arsen. atrophy of the kidneys, of the muscles, in general of the whole organismus, it depresses the spinal cord, and especially the sexual function, and its action is more lasting, i. e. its organic alterations arise slowly, but they act more deleterious. Its action is therefore more penetrating and powerful, as we will see in uræmia.

It is therefore accounted as a safe remedy in uræmic eclampsia under such conditions, as copper shows such eminent relations to the motor nerves, especially in persons of exquisitely fine and sensitive character, whereas Arsenic acts more on the sensory nerves. It is also a well-known fact, that Arsen. produces intermittent fever, Cuprum relapsing fever in irregular paroxysms; the more the latter localises itself in the liver, kidneys and spinal cord, the more will the symptoms correspond to Cuprum. It has peculiar, widely-ebbing remissions before a new impetuous paroxysm, distinct recurring attacks, emanating especially from the abdominal ganglia of the sympatheticus and from the vagus, as extraordinary primary foci of localisation the medulla oblongata and corpus quadrageminum, therefore its direct relation to the fossa rhomboidea, as deuteron intestines and kidneys. In obstinate vomiting, Cuprum am-moniato-sulphuricum is of benefit.

Otherwise again acts *Aurum muriaticum*, recom-mended already in 1840 by Huss and Liedbeck (Hygea 13). It affects next to the sudden specific blood-intoxication, primarily the left heart and with it the secreting tissue of the kidneys, i. e. the chief organ for the moving of the arterial blood, import of oxygen and the chief organ for secretion from it, export of nitrogen. Secondarily there arise from the affection of the heart (the heart contracts stronger and more frequently, the first sound of the heart is increased) on one side difficulty of breathing from stagnation in the pulmonary veins, the blood carrying organs before the circulation becomes checked, on the other side hyperæmia, after a while swelling of liver with altered secretion, a phenomenon entirely absent in arsenicum, and very slightly in phosphorus. Secondarily also through the affection of the kidney (they are decidedly hyperæmic, the pressure round the waist, the increased diuresis constant) symptoms arise in the bladder and neck of the bladder—by contact in consequence of the formed Carbonate of Ammonia symptoms of cerebral irritation from the infection of the blood (Carbonate of ammonia has been demon-strated in the brain during uræmia,) and manifestations in the mucous membrane of the eyes, nose and larynx. The frequent erections and the swelling of the testicles are a sympathetic phenomenon, caused by an increased diuresis, which emanated from renal hyperæmia, for we frequently observe increased

diuresis in high-graded lasciviousness. The excessive
loss of strength and the articular pains may be
caused by the changed nutrition of the spinal cord.

Inasmuch as Aurum quickly and forcibly acts
on heart and kidneys, a great loss of albumen must
certainly follow after a while, as is usually the case
in affections of the heart and kidneys, the blood thus
becomes poor in albuminous matter, in consequence
of which we find during a rapid course of the disease
and by prevailing localization of the morbid process
an asphyctic crasis from uræmia in the kidneys, or
with a general impoverishment of the blood degeneration of the exudation: from inanition, want of
albumen, young germinal cells (perhaps from a
surplus of alkaline salts, *Kletzinsky*) lose their power
to ripen into fibres, they granulate as cells in juicy
organs or after a short existence decay by passing
into ichor or necrosis, or they continue to granulate
as encephaloid neoplasma. Thus Aurum causes an
albuminous crasis, which necessarily finishes up as
hydræmia, as we see from the experiments of the
Austrian Provers' Union. Aurum thus corresponds
to M. B. and the consecutive hydrops arising from
gout, nephritic calculi, tedious suppurations, syphilis,
mercury or hepatic degeneration.

Such are the chief remedies, indicated in M. · B.
and its complications, their differential diagnosis is
exact and their selection therefore easy. Of secondary importance are the vegetables: Digit., Bryonia,
Helleb., Dulcam., Bellad., Atropin, Colchicum and
other remedies used in syphilitic albuminuria; other

remedies which need further chemical (and physiological) elucidation are metals and Kali bichr., Kali
nitr., natr. sulph., acid-benz., apis, lachesis.

Baehr, so well used to physiological criticism,
gives as a peculiar indication for *Digitalis* the apparently rheumatic pains so often met in parenchymatous nephritis and the catarrh of the lungs with its
characteristic copious serous secretion. If we only
judge digitalis by the scanty enumeration of its
symptoms, we fail in gaining any result. We have
to call analogy to our aid and say: all remedies
which disturb the arterial circulation in such a degree,
as the foxglove does, may also produce renal degeneration or at least albumen. Physiological experiments are necessary to decide, if the remedy acts
equally favorable in stasis emanating from disturbances of the lesser circulation. In fact a great many
special questions in our Materia Medica still await
their solution; how can we distinguish the sugar of
phosphor. acid and of lead in the urine? If digitalis
deserves the great praise bestowed upon it by
Bamberger in pneumonia without venesection, then
its specific relations to the kidneys through the veins
ought to be studied and physiology, formerly wrongly called toxicology, must decide whether this
consists in hyperæmia or also in exfoliation of the
epithelium. *Christison* witnessed twice beneficial
results from Digitaline; we once found the best
palliation from an infusum Digit. in an old woman
suffering from renal dropsy ex hypertrophia sinistra
cordis.

According to *Frerichs*, Digitalis increases the pressure of the fluid, which runs from the Malpighian bodies in the urinary canals, in order to remove all the coagula. Just as in their sphere Rhus and Puls. act differently on the blood, so we also find Spigelia and Digitalis diametrically opposed in their chief causes. We find good reason for their application, because according to their characteristics Aconite produces fibrinous phenomena, Spigelia albuminous, Digitalis hydræmic ones, whereas Puls. and Spig. have only this in common, that they easily produce medicinal aggravations, but they differ in their action on the heart as right and left, as Phosphor. and Arsen.

Spigelia generally produces rheumatic troubles (85–107, 300, 350, etc.), especially on the left side of the chest (320) also severe beating of the heart, which can be felt, heard and is externally visible, palpitation with pressure, anguish and oppression, heavy respiration, increased micturition. It is suitable in the beginning of left cardiac hypertrophy from rheumatic causes, in bellows murmur of the mitralis, in subacute inflammation of the Aorta with rheumatic and pseudorheumatic articular pains, the more so the less albumen and renal elements are found. Arsen. follows well after it.

Bryonia is a popular remedy in Styria and on the Rhine (Habscheid) in dropsies, and when given in too large doses produces pleuritis and peritonitis. We requested a physician to answer the question, how does Bryonia disturb the functions of the kidney? He emigrated to America, and after his

return he still owes us an answer. In spite of all
our labors, we cannot find in any proving a direct
action of Bryonia on the substance of the kidney, but
we can praise, with a good many others, its great
power of absorption in exudations of the serous and
fibrous membranes. Experience has taught us, that
it acts beneficially on renal concrements, but it
remains undecided, whether or not it affects directly
the kidneys, till we get physiological, and especially
chemical proofs. We use Bryonia only for a little
while in inflammations of serous membranes and for
their exudations.

Altschul recommends *Dulcamara* in M. B. from
cold; *Colchicum* before Arsen. is of value when
caused by damp dwellings, relapses after colds from
damp cold weather, in affections of the salivary
glands, bilious vomiting, suppressed perspiration,
(compare the provings of Unsin); *Aconite* is contra-
indicated even in the most severe fever, as it is not a
fibrinous one, but the protein-combinations prevail,
and hydræmia has either already set in, as in old
cases, or uræmia shows itself in acute cases, and then
we must distinguish between affections of the right
or left heart. Relapses of acute renal diseases in
consequence of catching cold are mostly fatal.

Let us not forget the use of narcotica, especially of
Opium, the chief remedy of the old school in all
acute and uræmic forms internally as well as by injections. By their intense action they may moderate
manifestations of sensitiveness, but they can only

5

profess a curative power, when they stand in direct
relation to the cause, as Bellad. to scarlatina.

The sovereignity of *Stramonium* in spasms, which
emanate from hyperæmia of the cerebral and spinal
membranes, as in cerebro-spinal meningitis without renal affection, or from nutritive disturbances
through the typhoid blood, where Stram. acts
better than Atropia, when the renal function is free,
may be omitted in the disease we speak of, as it
does not specifically change the kidneys, like e. g.
Bellad. (Eidherr). It costs too much labor for one,
who has little time to spare, to find out from the
provings of this and other remedies, like Apis, the
functional and organic disturbances of the kidneys
by chemical analysis. All vegetable remedies,
especially Bellad. and Atropine, are not the remedies
which promise favorable results in severe cases with
coarse organic alterations, though they may be more
favorable than we could expect from Morphine. In
recent cases of M. B. (less of uræmia) Atropine
(Bellad.) is certainly a great remedy for the congestive states of the kidneys, or of the liver from the
right heart, in neuralgia of the nerves of the head, in
nausea and vomiting, soporous cephalalgia, especially
where Uræmia passes over in Bright's disease;
Nicotine suits more in paralytic attacks, especially of
the abdominal ganglia.

The action of Bellad. and Atropine is under such
conditions evident, and if permitted to draw conclusions from light cases, the result may be called a
splendid one in comparison with the old school.

Arsen. follows well. In uræmic cases we immediately apply Arsen., without giving first Bell. We repeat, that Bellad. might become a sovereign remedy in moderate cases, but never Stram., Opium, or similar remedies. It is a wonder to us, how any one could recommend Morphine in eclampsia, when it is so clear, that a small dose of Phosph. is far more specific on account of its direct relation, and will act more favorably than a large dose of Morphine, which only shows that the prescriber does not know his Materia Medica.

The following is known of Mineral waters : Gastein (Proell) cured one case of renal degeneration in a phlegmatic patient, where albumen was present in large quantities; but where great irritability and incompatibility of character is combined with constant aggravation by eating, even in small quantities, then the prognosis for Gastein is more than doubtful.

Karlsbad is celebrated for diabetes, we never saw any benefit in M. B., although it retards hepatic granulations, and was therefore recommended from analogy, neither does it act well in albuminuria, and the same is the case with ferruginous springs. Frerichs sometimes recommends Vichy and Selters, the latter is at least a pleasant beverage, but they are by no means curative.

In epidemics of acute exanthemata Bright's disease follows frequently after scarlatina, more rarely after variola, and still more rarely after measles (in a large practice of many years I have only seen two cases of M. B. after measles). In all such cases we must

study closely the exanthema and the character of the
patient, the adjectives of the disease, for, although
the first desquamative symptoms in the kidneys
show themselves usually only in the beginning of
desquamation, still we find in some even light cases
during the eruption or immediately after it, œdema
of the face caused by a moderate nephritis, and this
at a time where the examination of the urine is hardly
thought of, although the kidneys, when their diseased
state is overlooked and thus no diagnosis made,
necessarily more quickly degenerate. Furthermore
scarlatina frequently is from the first day uræmic*
without paralysis of the vascular nerves, which
can only emanate from the Carbonate of Ammonia;
the dark urine already shows in the beginning of the
disease Ammonia, albumen and cylinders are absent
and appear when amelioration sets in, the patient
presents the picture of typhus, ileo-cœcal pain,
swelling of the spleen, even diarrhœa are mostly
absent—or scarlatina is simultaneously septic and
uræmic.

The specific remedies must be suited to the specific
cases. In scarlatina Bellad. is an old remedy and
tried prophylacticum; Helleborus is indicated, where

---

* Septic epidemics of scarlatina are rare, an uræmic one
was observed by us. A septic form happened 1818 in
Wallerstein, 1868, in the Jewish congregation of Munich,
without any influence upon the remaining population. In a
case where death set in the third day, Ammonia was found
in large quantities, from scarlatina, from the sepsis or from
both ?

we find albumen or even blood in the scanty urine, but we prefer Arsen. where renal elements arc present, and where chest and abdomen are more affected, whereas Helleb. shows more cerebral symp- toms. *Kafka* saw from Hepar after Bell. great benefit; we acknowledge never to have used the remedy. Where scarlatina begins with uræmic symptoms, Arsenic must be immediately given, or we risk, that the renal degeneration and alteration of the blood will increase, we have no time to change remedies, where the manifestations are so urgent, as in œdema pulmonum, and the rightly selected remedy must do quickly its duty. A complication with pneumonia might indicate Phosph. In septic epidemics of scarlatina we rely on the acids, especially muriatic-acid. In epidemics with tendency to M. B. we recommend the early application of arsenical preparations.

When typhus* is general, it will be frequently combined with renal degeneration; its epidemic appearance alone will frequently lead us to select arsenious and phosphoric acid, the latter of which Kammerer found of so much benefit for the same reason in diphtheritic laryngitis, which is frequently combined with M. B., but we must study all the remedies in every particular case.

No remedy in the last stage of the disease in drunkards can be of any benefit whatever, still we

* Andral found in forty-one typhus patients once, Becquerel in 38 cases 8 times M. B. Oppolzer observed it especially in typhus exanthematicus.

may try Bellad.,where the deliria, alternating with deep sopor, are of a frightful nature, with visions of spectres and persecutors; Arsen., where the restless anguish produces thoughts of murder ; Aurum in fear of death ; Calc.-ars. where the delirium mostly sets in during the evening and in the dark, hepatic cirrhosis is another indication for it, or for Cuprum, but never for China.

In M. B. from nephritic calculi Bryonia acts according to experience better than Natr.-carb. and Karlsbad. Turpentine enjoys an old reputation in calculi, but we cannot find any cases recorded in its favor. Where the calculus is large, angular and thus wedged in, remedies may prevent agglomeration, and thus facilitate their passage. During the colic, Bell., Atrop., Ars.

URGENT SECONDARY TROUBLES.

Among such let us enumerate chiefly at the beginning of the disease :

1. The sympathetic and reflectory morbid states of the diaphragm, which frequently make themselves known sooner than their cause, the M. B.; partial spasms of the diaphragm, hence vomiting with or without uræmia, require Cuprum ; inflammation of its serous membrane, Bryonia; Atropine stands between both, although the special indications of the remedies formerly mentioned, lose none of their importance.

2. During the further course of the disease œdema cerebri, œdema pulmonum 1 : 40, œdema glottidis 1 : 60, although comparatively rarely, may set in and in the lungs they mostly appear collateral. It is

none of our business, to put up a more reliable remedy against the tried Tartar-emetic, but we must prove, whether antimonials in general, and tartarus emeticus in particular are able to produce albuminuria in the kidneys. This we affirm unconditionally, although chemical and physiological experiments are still wanting, for C. Mayerhofer's article in Heller's Archive and Buchner's Jahrbuch der Pharmacodynamic is restricted to the degenerations of the liver, and and does not treat of the kidneys; so much is certain, that Tartarus produces bloody urine, thus at least renal hyperæmia and hæmorrhages of the Malpighian tufts; it has also been shown, that it can only secondarily affect the kidneys from the right heart, by keeping in view the eminent relations to the lungs, (it produces long coagula in the pulmonary arteries,) and we also know, that nobody will be attacked by an acute œdema pulmonum, whose right heart is perfectly normal. Tartarus therefore is the œdematous supplement to the albuminous phosphorus, when it also produces desquamation of the mucous membrane of the renal canals. In œdema cerebri Arsen. and Phosphor. are indicated under the conditions of right and left.

3. Hæmorrhage during parturition may arise from different causes, not rarely from relaxation of the renal capillaries and from nervous depression emanating from the spinal cord, in the latter case before uræmia and uræmic eclampsia breaks out; *we have never seen a case of uræmic eclampsia in the course of parturition, which was not preceded or followed*

by an increased hæmorrhage, whereas women advanced in years after having got over uræmia, may be attacked by hæmorrhages. That under such circumstances Ipec., China, Cinnamon. and other remedies are useless and application of cold injurious, is self-evident. Such cases need Phosph., Acid phosph., Arsen., Bell., according to their respective indications.

4. Among the urgent symptoms also belong the serous exudations and transudations in the beginning, in the middle and at the end; they are more frequent in albuminuria, whereas M. B. causes œdema in the most diverse parts of the body. Dropsy and œdema are only symptoms, by removing the cause, we remove the water; in acute cases certainly, in chronic ones slowly or not at all. It will always be hazardous, to fatigue an organ, whose functional power is reduced or nearly suspended.

URÆMIA.

Years ago we spoke of Uræmia as an adjectivum to the disease and as a condition to indicate the remedy, without being scolded by a Thersites, who wrongly considered himself injured, and will the semi-puritans now-a-days find a confounding specification in it, as in the syphilitic forms of Albuminuria? This might happen to physicians with a small practice, not to Agamemnon. Praise or vituperation do not touch us.

Uræmia is a severe symptom as a sequel of very different diseases, especially in epidemic scarlatina, *epidemics* of Cholera,* typhus, diphtheritis, in fermentation of urea in persons suffering from renal degeneration, in hyperæmia from dilatation of the spermatic veins during pregnancy, in puerperium and under all conditions, which generally produce Bright's disease.

Uræmia is toxæmia by Carbonate of Ammonia, which under certain conditions abnormally arises within the circulation, whenever the urea putrefies before its passage through the longitudinally stretched vessels of the renal pyramids, i. e. whenever it can draw one per cent. water in the reach of its formula, and we know now pretty well, what part is taken by certain parts of the brain, the fossa rhomboidea and corpus quadrageminum. The urine contains the Ammonia, but the *albumen is absent in acute cases*, which we must keep in mind, as albumen and other renal elements only appear during amelioration in the same proportion, as the Ammonia disappears. Just as the presence of pus, of putrid matter in the blood does not make pyæmia or septicæmia, so the presence of urea in the blood does not make uræmia. In both cases several conditions must be present, we need an incitor, a ferment.

Two views are taken about the origin of uræmia, a *functional* one (*Skoda, Buhl*) and a *chemico-vital* one (*Frerichs, Kletzinsky, Quaglio*), which we will note and reserve our mode of explanation for the particular forms.

---

* Acute intestinal Catarrh and Cholera are strictly distinguished by the quality of the urine, which in the latter case is that peculiar to M. B.

The first explanation is: It may be affirmed in regard to every acute Brightian degeneration of the kidneys, as in Cholera, that the urea remains in the kidneys, not only on account of the insufficiency of the kidneys, but also on account of the universally diminished peripheric molecular changes with all other products of decomposition in the tissues, and thus the kidneys are not alone to blame, but the simultaneous *acute atrophy of the brain* whenever uræmic phenomena show themselves.

A mechanical insufficiency of the kidneys for the secretion of urea exists only at that time, when a number of canals, especially of the tubular substance and there especially those of the little excrescences obliterate.　Other organs of secretions, especially intestinal tract and cutis, also the glands habituate themselves in chronic states not only to the excretion of water, but also of the urea, so that uræmic processes cannot gain firm ground.　The constant loss of albumen weakens the tissue-change, produces hydræmia and chronic atrophy of the organs, also of the brain.*　Under such circumstances, which may produce cerebral œdema, it is not always necessary to attribute it to decomposition of urea.　*Niemeyer* mentions perverse nutrition of the brain by the poisoned blood.　Whence arises this toxæmia, if not through the Ammonia?　Does the whole brain suffer

---

* *Landousi* already in 1850, defined Morbus Brighti as a cerebral disease.　In chronic cases of Uræmia without essential cardiac defects, we find towards the end great sleepiness caused by this atrophy, although no hydrops is present.

from this nutritive disturbance or does it prevail in certain parts? The answer is already before us, and is as follows: the chemico-vital mode of explanation, especially according to Kletzinsky and Quaglio, is: Uræmia arises, when the anomalous, qualitatively changed fibrine of the blood (it is softer and of less power of coagulation,) which is in a peculiar state of decay, shows its catalytic influence on the urea of the accidentally stagnated urine, whose normal secretion and excretion is rendered difficult or suspended either by the disease of the kidney or by another, even dynamic obstacle. Urea especially decays from contact with ferments, takes up water and becomes Carbonate of Ammonia. The latter, if not expelled by diuresis or diaphoresis, changes the hæmatine of the blood-cells, depriving it of the molecular binding power for the oxygen, and thus causes asphyxia, we find therefore in the height of the asphyctic stage of cholera the expired air nearly unchanged and the import of oxygen reduced to a minimum. How different the results of such asphyxia may be to the nerves, we may convince ourselves in the eclamptic uræmia of pregnancy and especially in the puerperium. The Carbonate of Ammonia of uræmic blood, does not only act as an asphyctic, but macerates and dissolves a part of the hæmatine and thus causes a dark color of the serum, which we again find in all normal transudations and produces the dark color of the skin in many typhoid processes, just as we see a bilious coloring of the conjunctiva in infarctus pulmonum, where it certainly does not depend on constituents of the bile.

Mobile azotic protein bodies, which in a state of molecular motion set up fermenting processes in stationary indifferent carbonaceous hydrates and in other matter, with which they come in contact act according to Kletzinsky as ferments, as instigators to putrefaction, as metabolic matter. The excrementitial urea begins to putrify, when, stagnated by disturbed excretion, it meets the catalytic power of an anomalous, loose, dissolving fibrine ; only accumulated urea is present in the blood ; a softer, retrogressively decaying fibrine meets it, and becomes itself a ferment and through propagation of its decay hands it over to hydratation, a negation to oxydisation and life.

Every action which produces fibrine, deprived of its power of coagulation, simultaneously with spastic contraction of the long branchless pyramidal capillaries, i. e. *obstructed transudation of the urea*, as cholera, typhus, or simultaneously with renal hyperæmia produces atony of the vascular tufts or exudation in the Malpighian tufts and in the straight linear urinary canals, i. e. *obstructed excretion of the urea*, as Arsen., Aurum, Phosphor., acute Bright's disease, eclampsia with dilated spermatic veins, carditis, etc., i. e. which produces by its stagnation contact of the urea with dissolute fibrine, may quickly or slowly have as a consequence that degeneration of the kidneys, which is usually called general uræmia.

According to this, uræmia may arise from two

chief causes : 1. Nutritive disturbance of a certain cerebral part near the corpus quadrageminum, to which Valentin first drew our attention, i. c. the fossa rhomboidea above the place, whose puncture causes diabetes, Buhl's cerebral atrophy, which with the prevailing anæmia of the parts does not exclude œdema, and 2, putrefaction of urea under the conditions already mentioned or to be mentioned. Without a ferment* the presence of urea in the blood does not act fatally (Christison, Rees). A man with far advanced granular degeneration of the kidney, was attacked with pericarditis without urœmic accidents, although his blood contained more urea than Frerichs had ever seen. But the intoxication may suddenly set in, when the patients still follow their occupation or are traveling.

All these noxious matters bear a specific relation to the secreting part of the kidneys, whose disturbed nutrition is the next cause of the stagnation of urea, although they may act only a secondary or tertiary part. They, like every other important morbific potency, select it at times and with certain individuals as place of deposit, passing by the primary homologous organ, or depositing themselves in its

* Infectious diseases, pregnancy and puerperium on account of the alterations in nutrition, diet (Herrich and Popp), medicaments which modify the tissue change, act as ferments. Animals, into whose veins Amygdalin is injected, may remain lively, but a single sweet almond suffices to flood their blood with prussic acid and oil of bitter almonds, and to poison them immediately.

neighborhood, and produce thus an anomalous direction, which in relation to the kidneys promote already present circulatory disturbances, as in tubercles, emphysema, pleuritic adhesions, in adhesions of the pericardium to the heart, in thin-walled or fatty degenerated heart, and also cause retarded circulation, so that the aorta never fills and the discharge from the renal veins is prevented, after having produced an atonic state of the capillaries. Typhoid blood, a decayed fibrine is also peculiar to them in pestilential or septic diseases, and the decomposition of the fibrine and the faculty of infection reaches its acme under the influence of heat and moisture—severe fever-heat—so that not rarely the beginning of the reactionary fever in the cholera, of the febrile storm in scarlatina, of the febrile exacerbation in carditis, is also the beginning of the putrefaction of the urea: the loose, during its decomposition constantly moving fibrine predisposes the urea to sudden dissolution through absorption of water.

Uræmia is thus no pathos sui generis, is impossible without the described alteration in the kidneys; and its group of symptoms imprints its marked stamp on every diseased state, which includes the conditions for the putrefaction of urea, so that with its first symptom a specific form, a *species* of a morbid type is clearly before us, which we denote as *uræmic*, may it manifest itself by asphyctic, comatose or eclamptic symptoms, as all of them arise from a common source, toxæmia from putrefying urine.

Cases of scarlatina, cholera, typhus, pneumonia,

nephritis, especially of pregnant women, have been observed, which had as prodroma more or less pronounced disturbed or suspended function of the kidneys, followed immediately or after hours or days by spasms similar to hysteric ones, or by coma with stertorous respirations under the form of cerebral torpor, and usually ending suddenly in death. According to the most frequent and striking phenomenon—the deep sopor—supposing them to be caused by the addition of some kind of typhus, they were described as *typhoids*, although here and there albumen and coagula were found in *nervous* pneumonia, in some *asthenic* measles, *typhoid* scarlatina, *septic* typhus, Cholera *typhoid;* in some cases of dry Cholera combinations of Ammonia were found in blood and urine, or in the exhalations of the lungs and skin. Adding such adjectiva to the disease, thus modifying the genera morbi or organic diseases, excluded the complication with others; but the identical predication always involved the same bases, usually looked for in a typhoid state, on account of the grave nervous disturbances. The convulsions, the *cerebral depression*, the acute cerebral atrophy of Buhl, the anæmia, the typhoid of such forms is only caused by the appearance of Ammonia in the blood, by the uræmic alteration of the crasis, as the manifold experiments on animals, especially of Frerichs, etc., with urea and carbonate of Ammonia, have decisively shown: after extirpation of the kidneys, the chief excreting organs for azot, in morbid cases for carbonate of Ammonia, and injection of urea in the veins, the functions and secretions remained intact 1–8 hours : (urea alone did not produce any morbid symptoms). Then the dogs became restless, staggered, vomited acid chyme or with an empty stomach mucous yellow masses with alkaline reaction, the *exhalation of the lungs showed Ammonia*, spasms convulsed them, which disappeared, returned and then passed over into constantly increasing stupefaction with snoring respiration, ending in death 2–10 hours after taking the urea; the blood contained large quantities of Ammonia, less the dark-red injected, urinous smelling stomach, less the bile and the other secretions, brain and cerebral membranes were intact, or we might say, not accessible to a fine examination. A solution of Carbonate of Ammonia, carried into the blood, immediately produced convulsions followed by coma with labored respiration (asphyxia), vomiting of bilious matter and surcharge of expired air with Ammonia, the latter accompanied the sopor, which lasted for hours, till both disappeared together, and after 5–6 hours the not nephrotomised animals again became lively and conscious. Not the Urea, but its hydratic product of decomposition is that which produces the phenomena characteristic of uræmia, just as we see in the human organism eclampsia, amaurosis, coma, as soon as stagnating urea putrefies, (when not present in the blood it is quickly exudated without any evil consequences.) This certainly is a most exquisite example of the origin of a deleterious noxa within the circulating vital element, as contrarily the poisoning by Carbonic acid in croup. He who cannot here distinguish between equal and similar, will make mistakes in the selection of the remedy.

Just like Alcohol the gaseous product of the putrefaction of urea reaches the cerebro-spinal fluid, and incites the nerve-centres in individually specific manner; either the brain, especially the fossa rhomboidea *depressing* (somnolence), or the spinal cord *stimulating* (convulsions, Asthma bronchiale · nervosum, uræmicum), the sympatheticus with its splanchnic ganglia and flexus *irritating:* sensation of goneness in epigastrio, profuse diarrhœa, vomiting, gushing out as from a pump, or *paralysing:* absence of all dejecta, of thirst, urine, etc. The latter mode may alone, by paralysis of the plexus cœliacus, become the cause of death, eclampsia only through simultaneous asphyxia or by soon following cerebral paralysis, the highest grade of narcosis, more rarely by acute œdema.

PATHOLOGICAL ANATOMY.

Anatomy fails to explain the alterations in the corpora quadragemina and in the central nervous system, whose functions are so frequently injured,— the cerebral atrophy is not proved de facto, only functionally. The only difference from M. B., is the fermentation of the urea, all other organic lesions are alike, neither anatomy nor microscopy gave us yet any safe indications about changes in the finely formed fossa rhomboidea which gives off the last branches to the vagus, and stands in direct connection with the aorta, the heart, etc. Guessing will not answer. We only know, that lesions of the fossa rhomboidea or its atrophy cause albuminuria.

In 20 cases, dying from convulsions and coma the brain and its membranes contained 8 times the normal quantity of blood, 4 times they were uræmic, 7 times the quantity of the fluid under the Arachnoidea was increased, 5 times unimportant, twice considerable, thrice the quantity of serum in the ventricles was increased, thrice membranes and substance of brain hyperæmic. When the stomach becomes the seat of severe attacks, its texture is not essentially altered, at other times slight ecchymosis are present in the mucous membrane, we mostly find moderate hyperæmia; in drunkards' chronic catarrhs. The intestinal canal, in spite of the profuse diarrhœas, remains unchanged, except in cholera, and we find exceptionally injection of the mucous membrane and follicular ulcers in the cœcum. The physical relations of the blood differ according to the stage of the disease, we find with the trabeculæ of the right heart stringy corded fibrinous coagula or tough ones or imperfect coagulation, really stagnation in the pulmonary arteries after abuse of Phosphor.; the smell gives us sometimes an ammoniacal fœtor, reminding one of putrid urine (Jaksch, Hammernick.) The blood contains Carbonate of Ammonia, whose quantity is very changeable, and also remnants of undecomposed urea. Functional disturbances are, however, seldom the object of study in the anatomical room.

DIAGNOSIS.

Urœmia is frequently only studied symptomatically, without giving full value to the causes of its phenomena and thus will be mistaken for meningitis cerebralis and spinalis (Schutzenberger*), apoplexia sanguinea et serosa, gastritis, typhus, carbonic acid intoxication, convulsions of different kinds, narcotic poisoning, pseudorheumatic pains, in other words, *urœmia may set in under most diverse forms.* Urœmic coma differs from bursting of morbid cerebral blood-vessels by the absence of paralysis of voluntary muscles, by a less slow pulse, quicker respiration and louder sound of its stertor, whereas the déep guttural sound in cerebral apoplexy arises by the swinging of the velum palati. The absence of the splenetic tumor, of the miliaria, the apathy, the quiet deliria, the cerebral torpor belong to urœmic fever, and not to typhus; the vomiting rich in ammonia, the somnolence, the stomach neither tympanitic nor painful, distinguishes the urœmic poisoning from gastritis. Urœmic narcosis is always accompanied by suppression of urine or by the secretion of a urine rich in ammonia and albumen with molecular detritus of the urinary canals, a condition absent in

---

* Urœmia might only be mistaken for meningitis in the very beginning, and the examination of the urine is the only sure method to determine the diagnosis, and this ought never to be neglected, as is so frequently the case. We might also examine the expired air. We should also be careful in chronic and urœmic forms, not to lay the blame on the pancreas on account of the vomiting.

carbonic acid narcosis, and in the coma produced by narcotica, without mentioning the specific actions of Hyosc., Stram., etc. The chemical quality of the urine alone gives us the diagnosis of an uræmic eclampsia in contradistinction to epilepsy, and to convulsions from other causes.

We distinguish in uræmia two kinds of urine, according as the disease arises from pre-existing Bright's disease, as in eclampsia, or where the disease is recent and spontaneous, as in eclampsia during scarlatina epidemics. In the former case we find with the albumen and renal elements Ammonia, in the latter only ammonia with scanty urinary secretion. The latter circumstance has caused many quarrels and false ideas in the diagnosis as well as in the therapeutics, as if M. B. could not be present without albumen, which is certainly the case in all acute and recent forms of uræmia as in analbuminosis.

We recognise in chronic cases the fermentation of the urea and urates, and their decomposition and import in the blood: a, by the increase of the symptoms, severe headache, vertigo, deafness, amaurosis, vomiting, spasmodic and eclamptic paroxysms, sopor, etc. b, by the frequent, but not always sudden disappearance of the albumen in the scantily passed urine. c, by the presence of ammonia in smaller or larger quantities.

Scarlatina and eclampsia may from the very start set in as recent uræmia, and only after amelioration has begun, albumen and renal elements appear as symptoms of M. B. Renal degeneration in scarlatina usually appears only when desquamation begins, and in but a few cases can molecular detritus or albumen be found in the first days.

Urine, containing ammonia, reacts the more alkaline, the more Ammonia is present, smells of it and causes the precipitation of the earth-phosphates, which in combination with the Ammonia precipitate in clear crystals. We recognise Carbonate of Ammonia: a, by the smell, b, by the alkaline reaction and by the fumes, when heating the urine; we take a small retort, and put through the cork a glass tube of the size of a quill. We pour a few drops of urine in the retort, and put in the glass tube red litmus-paper, moistened with distilled water, which then turns blue. By such an experiment we also distinguish between urine, alkaline from Carbonate of Ammonia, and urine turned alkaline by the too frequent use of vegetable acids. c, by the development of Carbonic acids in beads, by effervescence, in high grades by foaming on the addition of an acid, for the practical physician we recommend Nitric-acid. d. A sediment forms of phosphoric Ammoniac-magnesia and of urate of Ammonia, as the Carbonic acid partially escapes from the Ammonia, and the urea is added to it.

In addition to the chemical proof, we possess the following symptoms in the complex of uræmic intoxication, for the transformation of the urea into carbonate of Ammonia: frequently reduced or suppressed secretion of urine, coming on without warning or discharge of only small quantities, reminding one of jaundice, the urine becomes at first bloody, turbid, rich in albumen, when the increase of exudations in the urinary canals (the transudation of urea in them and their excretion is stopped, stagnant and putrefies) sets in with full force as cerebral torpor or as spinal irritation, producing exquisite functional changes in the nervous system, so that we witness either one alone or both together.

It would seem, that thus the diagnosis should be very easy, and still there are cases, where even the most skillful physician will remain in doubt, as in far advanced stages of eclampsia, where it is difficult to decide, whether cerebral atrophy is present or cerebral œdema, which we cannot imagine without anæmia of the cerebral substance, although in such a case our choice vacillates between right and left, between Arsen. and Phosph., and finally atrophy as well as anæmia favor watery transudations. In such difficult cases the practical tact of the physician only can decide. We do not find here the well-known consensus between heart and kidneys, but between brain and kidneys. Just as we have studied, whether hypertrophy of the heart or Bright's disease is primary, so here, whether cerebral atrophy or uræmia. Till Valentin's views are more thoroughly examined, we consider the atrophy, the anæmia of the brain as secondary manifestations, and we are led to such a conclusion by the morbid states of the kidneys during pregnancy.

PROGNOSIS.

Of 436 patients, suffering from M. B., 116 cases

were of uræmic origin.* In most of them the
uræmia is ephemeral and can be cured, especially
when still recent and immediately diagnosed, which
is of the highest importance e. g. in epidemic scarlatina, which in its uræmic form immediately on the
first day looks like typhus, as the skin then shows
no eruption and it cannot be unimportant to allow
the Ammonia-poisoning to remain undisturbed for
hours; Uræmia runs a more unfavorable course in
eclampsia of pregnancy, of parturition and of lying-in
women, if arising from an already existing renal degeneration; more favorably, when appearing at least
without preceding renal lesion; nearly absolutely
fatal in the paralytic form of cholera (Nicotine according to Wurmb), slowly killing in the cholera without
the cold stage. It will be easily understood, that
changes in other organs must be the more unfavorable,
the coarser they are. More anon in the respective
forms of uræmia.

Uræmic forms in lying-in women, in pregnancy,
with slight organic lesions, mostly run a favorable
course, when M. B. did not exist too long, or when
acute cerebral atrophy or œdema is not also simultaneously present.

FORMS OF URÆMIA.

There is only *one* Morbus Brighti, but it may
appear in different forms according to the adjectiva

---

* The frequency of the uræmic beginning of the diseases
corresponds in numbers, but not in condition to the hypertrophy of the left heart.

of the disease, i. e. according to the constitution of the patient; there is also only *one* Uræmia, but it manifests itself in various forms, and we may distinctly distinguish four forms: the *comatose* in scarlatina, measles, intermittent fever, genuine M. B., Cholera-typhoid (when the cerebrum is œdematous or anæmic, Traube); the *eclamptic* in pregnancy, puerperium, hypertrophy of the thymus, hooping-cough, (when the middle parts of the brain are anæmic, Traube); *the asphyctic* in asiatic cholera, myocarditis; *the paralytic* in some epidemics of cholera, in lying-in women.

The setting in of uræmia is so terrible and sudden, on account of the blood-asphyxiating, and secondarily the nerve-centres attacking action of the Carbonate of Ammonia, even to the destruction of the electrotonus, that it alone, as the momentarily urgent indicatio vitalis and not the prior disease, determines the choice of the remedy.

In the first, the *narcotic or comatose* form, the patient at once or after headache, vertigo, nausea, vomiting, all lasting only a little while, falls in a deep sopor with or without amaurosis and deafness, to which is soon added hurried and stertorous respiration, with pale face,* immovable empty gaze and normal pupil with feeble reaction to light, or with circumscript,

---

* The uræmic stertor differs from the apoplectic one, there are not the deep guttural sounds from the vibrations of the velum palati, but louder sounds, from the shock of the expired air against the palate and lips.

frequently one-sided vermillion-colored cheeks, frightened expression of the face, dark injected conjunctiva and lids glued together by puriform mucus.

Such a coma kills in the first days by cerebral atrophy, or by cerebral œdema and anæmia of solitary parts of the brain, by œdema pulmonum, by hypostasis from disturbed innervation of the circulatory organs, or by a combination of such accidents; but usually the sopor wears off, and health is restored in two or three weeks after repeated paroxysms of narcosis, and never till the urinary secretion becomes again regular with strongly smelling perspiration and returning ease of respiration, or the causal disease, which produced the urinary putrefaction, makes other secondary deposits without further uræmic manifestations, and thus perfect health is not restored.

The importance of eclampsia,* which *Rayer* considers albuminous, *Frerichs* uræmic, in contradistinction to that eclampsia, emanating from the cerebral and spinal nerves without alteration of the kidneys, deserves our special attention, especially as also Kilian and others affirm: no eclampsia without uræmia.† The whole quarrel between the followers

---

* Eclampsia in puerperium and pregnancy happens once in 425 cases, according to Madame Lachapelle once in 200 cases. Beigel found in 13 cases four times M. B., once endometritis, 3 times œdema pulmonum, 3 times œdema cerebri, no changes whatever in three cases.

† Lever found in 10 cases of eclampsia nine times large quantities of albumen, once meningitis. Convulsions may arise in some cases from it or from loss of blood and hysteria. The diagnosis is easy.

of Scanzoni and Frerichs may be easily settled by
the following axiom, especially by keeping in view
the already described state of the brain: the degeneration of the kidneys either existed already, when
the eclampsia set in, and then we can easily demonstrate with the albumen at least decided traces of
Ammonia, or it is entirely recent, shows therefore
no albumen whatever with the traces of Ammonia
and with the detritus from the Bellinian tubuli;
cylinders and albumen do not precede the acute
disease, but follow it, wherefore many have denied
any causal connection, because they have neglected
microscopical examination (Braun, Letzmann). Thus
at least the cause of the disease is clear, as even
Scanzoni admits, that cholæmia and uræmia may
give rise to convulsions by their influence on brain
and spinal cord. Hesse, who in all such cases
observed changes in the kidneys, remarks, that
eclampsia must not necessarily follow under such
conditions, but it also needs a certain state in the
cerebral substance, and an incitor for the putrefaction
of the urine or both.

When the process in the kidneys does not reach
that height, that the excretion of urea is essentially
obstructed by it, no convulsions follow; more than
half of the patients suffering from albuminuria are
thus spared. Devilliers and Regnauld observed in
20 pregnant women with albuminous urine nine
times eclampsia.

The eclamptic form, mostly caused by mechanical
stagnation of the venous circulation in the abdominal

cavity, is characterised by sudden convulsions, similar to epileptic ones, which, vibrating through the whole muscular system, abate for a time, to rage with new force, with labored breathing and undisturbed consciousness, but more frequently with intense stupefaction, in which the clonic spasms become lost. The twitchings of the extremities frequently alternate with spasms of the diaphragm, or of the bronchial and laryngeal muscles, making themselves known by widely diffused ronchi, cyanosis, suddenly obstructed respiratory movement, interrupted or followed by shrill, long-drawn frequently returning screams, without cough or aphony. Intermission of the spasm fails to produce cession of the sopor; the former returns, till after repeated paroxysms stupor with snoring breathing—cerebral atrophy, oedema, uræmic paralysis—either soon closes the scene, or the patient recovers his faculty of thinking, complains of debility, dull headache, dull sight without any recollection of the preceding paroxysm. Analogous to the cardialgic vomiting in myelitis we frequently witness before and with the eclampsia as reflex of the spinal irritation an activity of the vascular nerves as branches of the sympatheticus and a hyperæsthesia of the large abdominal plexus—neuralgia cœliaca, etc., with deathly anguish, fainting, obstructed diaphragmatic breathing, thirst, suspended secretion of urine and bile, hyperæmia from stagnation in the gastro-intestinal membrane with vomiting or diarrhœa, as a consequence of the spastic narrowing of the capillaries.

The uræmic headache, an emanation of the dyscrasic irritation of the brain, which sometimes precedes the sopor, is in intensity perfectly alike to the neuralgic one, but raging without intermissions, and frequently depriving the patient of his senses; it disappears with the setting in of coma or of profuse urinary or perspiratory secretion.

Vomiting is sometimes constant, discharging half-digested ingesta, followed by tough mucous masses, mixed with bile or watery, neutral or alkaline reacting substances, containing Ammonia. Its cause is not the Ammonia, not the increase of activity of the posterior crura of the diaphragm from nephritis, but the influence of the decomposed blood on the nerve-centres. It ceases, as soon as atrophy of the kidneys or of the brain sets in.

The spasm of the dilators of the vocal chords, and still more that of the bronchial muscles belongs to the most frequent signs of uric putrefaction, never reaches the height of the spasm of the vagus-branches in hooping-cough or in hypertrophy of the thymus, but in connection with the headache and with the eclampsia, it may be taken as a most distressing accident, aggravating for a time the prognosis of the kidneys and of the heart.

The *pulse* is not altered, during the sopor only harder, during the convulsions on account of the disturbed breathing accelerated, often irregular, and again normal during the intervals; but uræmia may lengthen itself to a torpid fever, with small, soft, frequent pulse, dry hot skin, brown dry tongue, nauseous vomiting, excessive debility and apathy, ending in coma, stupor, subsultus tendinum and closely resembling typhus. Thus febris uræmica makes itself known by scanty urine, containing albumen, fibrinous coagula or emulsive balls, smells like hippuric acid and is of dark yellow color. A slow reconvalescence is the rule.

The symptoms of uræmia frequently form the first indications of established M. B., and its decline is mostly introduced by profuse critical urinary excretion. Carbonate of Ammonia will be discharged by the stomach, by the skin, kidneys and lungs, so that vomiting, anasarca, profuse transpiration and diuresis, if following in the course of uræmic diseases, retard or prevent the development of nervous phenomena, and if the expired air is measured for Carbonate of Ammonia, we may find out the degree of poisoning. Inflammations set in during eclampsia as puerperal complications, or pneumonia, pleuritis, peritonitis run an unfavorable course.

Simple coma and the eclampsia with or without narcosis have most frequently been observed in sudden suppression of the urinary discharge during pregnancy, in cholera, typhus, scarlatina, as in such a case rotten fibrine causes putrefaction and decomposition of the blood in the urea, which became stagnated by far advanced renal exudations.

In eclamptic and comatose uræmia of a lesser grade, the prognosis is not absolutely unfavorable; it may pass off and perfect restoration ensue, when the alterations in the organs, exporting the azote, did not last too long, but it may kill in a few hours or days* by over-irritation, or by direct extinguishment of the energy of the animal nervous system in its centres, and no other cause can then be found, than the renal degeneration.

More rapidly and more destructive is the course of the two other forms of uræmia, *the asphyctic and the paralytic*, the former by genuine paralysis of the blood, (death of the blood-cells, extinguished capacity of the hæmatine to bind the oxygen, and to render the blood-juice bright red and vivifying) and by paralysis of the circulatory organs, (muscles of heart and arteries), the latter by paralysis of the splanchnic plexus of the sympatheticus, especially of the vasomotory nerves and of the muscular coat of the stomach and intestines.

Both forms produce death by inanition of oxygen, showing itself by torpor and *paralysis of the central organs of vegetative life*—heart and nerve ganglia.

As the continuous stimulus of oxygen in a steady flow of bright-red arterial blood, is indispensable to the brain and nerve mass in order to carry out their functions, and as probably every nervous affection emanates from the blood, by abstraction of oxygen (by tying an artery, we stop the mechanical and physical stimulus, we alter the molecular state and the electrotonus, we change the biochemical and material mixture of the brain and nerve mass, all of which making itself manifest by disturbances in mobility and sensibility, in coldness, numbness,

---

* Lever lost 44 in 166, Devilliers 11 in 20, Hunter supposes that more than half will die.

muscular trembling in the extremity, whose artery was ligated,) so we see in this form of uræmia, the extremely asphyctic action of the Carbonate of Ammonia on the blood-cells produces a more or less acute or slower cessation of the activity of the heart, this centre of the blood's motion, and we can easily explain all the phenomena of uræmic asphyxia from such alteration of this focus : in the nervous life narcosis, in the blood-life asphyxia. Without reaction, without excretion of Ammonia, brain, ganglia, heart are torpid, especially in the vasomotor nerves, therefore *hyperæmia by stagnation.*

In the asphyctic form the plexus cardiaci and the muscles of the arteries are not any more enlivened by oxygen, they steadily contract with less energy, the impulse of the heart becomes less distinct, the pulse smaller, as in carditis the heart cannot propel the pulmonary blood in the arteries, stagnation in the venous circulation arises, cyanosis with oppression in the chest and a feeling of anguish, which, in connection with the abolished electrotonus of the brain, suddenly, like a lightning flash, prostrate in exquisite cases the patient, so that he falls down, as in an apoplectic fit, with staring eyes and loss of voice ; soon after the first symptoms of poisoning reaction sets in, with quicker and broader beat of the heart and pulse, and as a reflex reaction, with spasms in the chest and calves of the legs. But as the blood-cells still fail to act, the reaction is of short duration, the paralysis of the heart, the obstruction in the circulation progresses, dyspnœa and hunger for air increase from the obstructed change of the blood in the capillaries of the pulmonary alveoles, the diffusion of the gases, respiration, does not take place, as the lungs, in spite of full expansion of the chest and in spite of free entrance of air in the alveoli, return that air in a perfectly unchanged form.

Consequences of accumulation and thickening of the blood in the veins are : sinking of the temperature, diminished reflex irritability, slight filling of the left heart and of the large arteries, therefore *diminution of urinary secretion and thirst.* With all the anguish of death, the apnœa and the constant restlessness, the mind remains unclouded to the last, no coma sets in, but the great apathy is remarkable, the carelessness in such a dangerous state, headache only rarely, but frequently dimness of eyes, surring in the ears, vertigo, it is in fact a gradual extinction of the patient, even the tracheal rattling before death is absent, which sets in in 6 to 24 hours. In rare cases, health may be restored with copious excretions of sweat and urine, under gradual disintegration of the stagnation in the circulation, and with returning tonus in the muscles of the heart and arteries ; but also a reactionary fever, followed by inflammatory states, especially of serous membranes, denotes the time, when the deleterious matter is discharged, and the vivifying atmospheric oxygen reenters the black tarry blood.

The *paralytic* form runs its fatal course still quicker, as with the acute paralysis of the heart, and with the emanations of every high-graded uræmia, we have also here a perfect functional suspension of the abdominal sympatheticus with the following phenomena: entire absence of all dejecta and secreta, although a transudation of serum through the atonic capillary walls, in the glands and submucous tissue of the intestinal mucous membrane is present, absence of thirst and of pain, pulselessness, suspension of reflex activity, frog-like skin, symptoms which alone would suffice to produce a fatal issue in a short time, but in connection with asphyxia they absolutely render a fatal prognosis.

THERAPY.

The symptoms and their causes are the disease, but the disease also is the complex of symptoms, and ensures the diagnosis of the disease, or the recognition of the causes of the disease. The synthesis deserves preference to that of analysis in a rational diagnosis of a remedy, especially in processes devoid of symptoms, or rich in general sympathetic symptoms. The disease always remains the same, but constitutions differ. The essential differential characteristic manifestations, are based on the *ætia* (causes) and *adjecta* of the disease; the meeting of disease and remedy, and their mutual resolution through the similarity of their characters (their causes), as the principle of a homœopathic or individually specific therapy, is contained in the definition of the simile: *similar in appearance, different in their causes, involving the contrarium.*

We diagnose the remedy by individualizing the

6*

disease, the characteristic epitheton, whether diphtheritic, croupous, catarrhal; not the morbid substantive the angina, decides the choice of the remedy, not the uræmia, but its form and complication. Asthma from thinning of the right heart, from diaphragmatic atrophy, from bronchiectasy, from organized exudation of the spinal cord, from neurosis of the vagus, from uræmia, from arthritic deposits on the cardiac valves, only as slightly differ in their symptoms as obstruction from atony of the intestinal mucous membrane, from torpor of the muscularis coli, recti, from carcinomatous intestinal structure differs from invagination, from intestinal adhesion, etc. The similar causes alone, expressing themselves in similar effects, in similar stimulus or torpor on vagus, cardiac nerves, medulla spinalis, muscularis intestinorum, sympatheticus, etc. are the symptoms, whence cometh an unerring diagnosis of the remedy.

As a design for the outlines of uræmic therapy we take as characteristic hints the forms, under which we find the disease, i. e. the places of deposits for the Ammonia conditional to the individual, but especially the anatomical substratum of the phenomenon, the specific alteration of the nutritive and functional disturbance of the kidneys, also the asphyctic crasis, the coaffection of the vagus and of its origin in the brain.

As chief-remedies correspond to uræmia generally, produce dissolution of the fibrine and accumulation of urea in blood, i. e. putrefiers of urea: *Arsen.*, *Cupr.*, *Phosph.*, *Aurum*, *Terebinthina.* They correspond rather to the blood-crasis, specifically altered by the product of the putrefying urea, the Carbonate of Ammonia, whereas *Prussic-acid* and *Nicotine* correspond to the uræmic asphyctic crasis, inasmuch as they produce a nearly similar asphyxia of the blood-cells.

The remedies of the first class, although they all produce stagnation and putrefaction of urea, differ greatly among themselves; to determine this difference, no matter whether we attribute it to the cerebral atrophy or the Ammonium as primum movens, is the sole thema of a rational therapy; everything else is of no practical value. Whether we are able to do justice to such a work, is difficult to decide, as a differential diagnosis only exists since Wurmb. Arsen., Phosph., Aur., etc. produce accumulation of urea first of all through obstructed excretio urinæ: the exudation in the · Malpighian tufts produced by them, its shifting towards the capsule of Muller, the exudation in the urinary canals fills the latter more or less with inorganizable matter, so that the urine, which continues to be secreted, cannot be moved forward fast enough ; later with the return of normal nervous activity with the loosening and final detrition of the mucous membrane of the urinary canals and of the vascular tufts, which undergo a kind of paralysis with even a small quantity of albuminous exudation and thus become more or less incompetent to carry on their functions or through the quantity of albuminous coagulation in the small glands of the mucous membrane, as Phosphor. also causes the same in the right heart and pulmonary arteries, they lose the power to carry away the excrementitial parts of the blood, urea, uric-acid, etc. or to make normal urine; Cuprum, on the contrary, although it causes a high-graded hyperæmia of the secreting renal parenchyma, as can be seen after the use of candies colored by it, thus producing albuminuria, accomplishes the accumulation of urea immediately by suspending its transudation in consequence of the intensive irritation, even spasm of the nerves supplying the renal blood-vessels, which ensues from primary irritation of the sympatheticus, thus more of the animal life. It is true, that after a continued action on the contraction of the blood-vessels their relaxation, stasis, follows and with the exudation simultaneous closing up of the tubuli uriniferi, as in the former case, but the character of erethismus, of the sudden attack, especially of the abdominal plexus of the sympatheticus, of the vagus and of the recurrens, with the consequent sensation of destruction without the power of resistance, of a kind of irregular occurrence of the symptoms, which appear in groups, with a paresis, immediately following the spasm, the reflected seizure of the corpora quadragemina (fossa rhomboidea), the metastatic affection of the cerebrum, *especially of the tenth pair of cerebral-nerves*, the secondary seizure of the hepatic cells, distinguishes the Cuprum-disease from the Arsenic-disease with its quantity of stormy reactionary signs, which equally annoying the left heart and renal arteries, directly produces intensive fluxion and inflammation of the urinary canals by specific irritation of the nerves of the renal capillaries, in constant contradiction to the torpor of the action of Gold and Turpentine, which also produce direct atony of the renal capillaries, hyperæmia by stagnation and exudation of the Bellinian tubuli. The uric putrefaction of Arsen. and Aurum produces coma, that of Cuprum eclampsia. The narcotic form of uræmia arises from direct depression of the brain in Aurum, from hyperexcitation and final cerebral torpor in Arsen. from atrophy in Phosphor. and the convulsive form of uræmia originates in the immediate irritation of the Carbonate of Ammonia on the medulla spinalis.

Another mode of attack in Cuprum is the undulating one, as in some narcotic medicaments, thus the irritation of the vascular nerves, torpor, followed by tension of the vascular coat, relaxation with hyperæmia from stagnation, transudation followed by exudation, surcharge of the blood with carbon, cyanosis, emaciation, coldness, slow circulation.

Especial indications for Cuprum are: renal hyperæmia or hypostasis with reflex action in the motory sphere; such renal alterations arise from neuroses of the ganglia of the sympatheticus on a melanotic basis; neuralgia, hysteria, intermittent fever or from processes with hyperglobulosis and deposit in the abdominal viscera: pregnancy, cholera, plethora; in the first case the paroxysm per se causes spasm of the vascular nerves and renal fluxion with attenuated, limited or suspended urinary secretion and stagnation of the urea, in the second the inspissation of the blood and the change of hydrostatic proportions of the renal vascular apparatus causes increased tension of the vascular walls and after a while exudation of albumen, accumulation of urea, just as it also produces cramps in the calves of the legs by interruption of the conductibility of the electric current between neurilem and nerve-cord, so far only peculiar to Cuprum and to M. B. in cholera. In uræmia, suitable to Cuprum, the convulsions, the nervous asthma alternate with talkative delirium, with thoughts chasing one another, interrupted by amaurosis or difficulty of hearing, and the severest paroxysms are followed by apathy, intense indifference even to death. During the paroxysm the face is distorted, frequently reddened, the eyes protruding, staring, the spasm of the extensors prevailing, tongue and respiration cold, pulse little altered, the long-drawn screams forced, without painful sensation, till exhaustion, sweat, stupefaction comes on and the spasm draws to a close. : The physician, especially the homœopathic one, is frequently called at so late a stage of the eclamptic disease, that at the utmost he may only be able to diagnose uræmia, but not, whether atrophy or œdema of the brain is present, which is of such vast importance in the selection of the remedy, as the choice of the remedy in both cases—setting aside the presence of heart-disease—greatly differs, still a homœopathic physician might be able to save the case, given up by other schools. But we candidly acknowledge, that at the acme of the disease we are unable to give differential characteristics, and entirely rely on our practical sense to distinguish between atrophy and œdema of the brain. (In nucc our general therapy would read thus : paroxysmal eclampsia : Cuprum ; serosity of the brain : Arsen.; atrophy of the brain : Phosph.)

Phosphorus differs from the versatile Arsenicum and from the eclamptic, and finally depressing Cuprum, by its copious albuminous blood-coagulation in the right heart and in the lesser circulation (according to experiments of Liedbeck,* Buchner, Wurmb,) and this in a far greater degree than we find it in Tartenuet., which also acts paralyzingly in the same degree on the adnexa, producing fibrinous deposits, which process we first witness in the renal veins, secondarily in the arterial system, finally and chiefly by the kind of acute atrophy, which it produces in the brain and medulla oblongata in contradistinction to the watery transudation, produced by Arsen. in the brain. As Arsenicum generally represents the curative remedy for the narcotic form, and Cuprum for the eclamptic form, so Prussic-acid and Nicotine, this preformed alkaloid free from all oxygen, are the representatives of the highest grade of the asphyctic form of uræmia. Related remedies must present contrasts, thus Ipecac. and Veratr., thus Cupr. and Nicot., irritation and torpor, spasm and paralysis, erethism and want of reaction. Nicotine and prussic acid are very nearly alike in their asphyxiating power, suspending the oxygenation of the blood, but the result of this inanition of oxygen differs according to the organs

---

* De veneficio phosph. acuto; Upsalæ, 1845.

homologous to each of them. The want of oxygen expresses itself first, and especially with hydrocyanic acid in diminished energy of the activity of the heart ; the beat of the heart is accelerated with a full and soft pulse, with a gradually slower and weaker motion of the blood, stagnation of blood follows in the heart and lungs, palpitations with indescribable anguish and oppression of the chest, venous accumu-lation of the blood in the abdomen and liver, depression of the sensibility of the irritable organs, manifestations of the greatest relaxation of the nerves, first convulsions, then paralysis of the muscles, extreme apathy, also thick fluid, oily, blue-black blood, anxious labored respiration, slow moaning breathing, tracheal rattling, laryngeal paralysis or sudden paralysis of the heart.

Homologous to Nicotine are the abdominal portion of the sympatheticus, and the ganglia of the base of the brain with the medulla oblongata. Nicotine uræmia is therefore distinguished next to its asphyxia, which is of double origin, (cardiac paresis from weakened function of the vagus from the medulla oblongata, and paralysis of the blood-globules from Carbonate of Ammonia), especially by torpor of the abdominal ganglia, or paralysis of some plexus of the sympatheticus, e. g. of the diaphragm, and we find therefore as the most preeminent phenomena of Nicotine uræmia thirstlessness, absence of all reaction, indifference to everything even to death, cold forehead, absence of vomiting and of diarrhœa in spite of copious transudation masses in the abdominal tract, more or less total paralysis of the intestinal coats and of the muscular coat of the arteries, absence of all secretion from liver and kidney and death, far quicker than in any other form of uræmia. Nicotine uræmia arises differently from that of Arsen., with the nearly universal paralysis of the ganglia of the sympatheticus and of the vascular nerves, the walls of the blood-vessels in the renal artery and tufts are naturally more or less paralyzed; the next consequence is diminished motion of the blood, stagnation of it and of the urea; the stagnated urea finds within the blood-vessels a fibrine destroyed by the Nicotine, and thus necessarily finishes quickly its chemical change to Carbonate of Ammonia.

It is self-evident, that all remedies, already mentioned under M. B. may also be of use in this disease.

Cases of uræmia, running a favorable course, begin with vomiting (and diarrhœa), for which the old school gives opium and its salts. The uræmic vomiting which Christison stopped with kreasote, naturally needs no symptomatic treatment for its amelioration, but we have only to notice its chief cause and the points, through which they make themselves known, thus Cuprum, Arsen., Phosph., and their different preparations under the conditions already mentioned. When the vomiting is connected with diseases of the stomach, pancreas or liver, one or the other of these heroic remedies fully suffices, according to their specific relations, in ulcer of the stomach Arsen. and Phosph., in intestinal hæmorrhages during typhus Arsen., in gastric hæmorrhage from denudation of the coronaria Phosph., in hepatic cirrhosis cuprum, in pancreatic affections Calc-arsen., etc., etc.

If it is the work of Materia Medica, to study the actions of noxæ on healthy persons and animals, and to judiciously apply the recent advancements in Chemistry, Microscopy and physiology, then it will be the duty of a therapy not only to give all the remedies for certain diseases, but also to prove, how the similar ones differ one from another. We have tried it for uræmia, may others decide how far we have succeeded. A few words more about Albuminuria.

ALBUMINURIA.

Albuminuria* is according to our observation in syphilis of the kidneys, in renal or intestinal concre- . ments that spontaneous, but mostly as in old cardiac

---

* The medicinal rheumatism of Schœnlein is perhaps yet remembered by many. Recent authors fall in the same error and speak of a lead and silver albuminuria, and fail to distinguish between pathology and toxicology. Only diseases, requiring such energetic remedies, show such important functional disturbances of different organs, which may easily have albuminuria in their train, and no mortal will be able to prove, whether the organic lesion or the abuse of the remedy is most to blame for the renal degeneration, for we do not study physiology on the sick, nor pathology on the healthy. Every one may therefore draw his own conclusions.

therefore affected from the left heart, or the Bellinian diseases symptomatic chronic functional disturbance of the kidneys, in the secretion of which only albumen shows itself as a foreign element, with an entire absence for a time of all renal elements, mentioned under M. B., although they may have been present at a former period, or in other words, the presence of Morbus Brighti is characterized by renal detritus and albumen, that of albuminuria by albumen alone, and both differ from uræmia by the Ammonia, with or without the presence of renal elements and albumen, although one form may pass over into another.

We usually find 0,2–3,4 per cent. albumen, daily 2–25 grm. Most frequently we find this form of disease in persons, who recovering from acute albuminous nephritis, from uræmia, repeatedly expose themselves to well-known deleterious influences, or who have not fully recovered, or who from whatever cause suffer from continued arterial hyperæmia or venous stasis of the kidneys, as is the case in gonorrhœic blenorrhœa of the bladder. The excretion of albumen is also favored by greater lateral pressure, showing itself most clearly in the Malpighian tufts, by less celerity in the blood, or by a watery condition of the blood. *Albumen never appears for any length of time, without clearly demonstrable disorganizations in the kidneys*, and hyperinosis excludes this affection.* The Malpighian tufts are

* An incidental albuminuria, which causes no further substantial changes is met in trauma of the renal region, during the use of Cantharides, in fibrinous nephritis.

120 MORBUS BRIGHTI.

tubuli from the right heart or from the vena cava ascendens, without desquamation, which certainly preceded in ¼ of all cases, also of all uræmic ones, without counting other acute diseases. An essential factor of the molecular detritus, which is now absent, was formerly present, though perhaps only in a slight degree, or it may reappear or the epithelial glands undergo a slow fatty degeneration without detritus.

The question is close at hand: may albuminuria transform itself again to perfect M. B., just as des-quamation continues as albuminuria? With the materials before us we may affirm it thus: Albumi-nuria passes only rarely into M. B. and then only under the form of subacute uræmia, or during ec-lampsia in the most acute M. B; it may happen in hyperæmia of serous membranes, especially of the pleura, with severe neuralgic manifestations in the head (Occip. and Trig.) and simultaneous renal affec-tion, so that the blood-globules are prevented by two factors from fixing the oxygen, and a grand reflex from alienation of nervous activity allows no time to be lost.

Another question still waiting its decision, is: does loss of albumen only take place in M. B. or do also other organs with inviolability of the kidneys secrete a large quantity of albumen, analogous to the process of the kidneys. We only know of two sure examples of ascites with large quantities of albumen, which could be referred to syphilis and use of Mercury; cases of M. B. and simultaneous large quantities of albumen in ascites have several times been reported. What changes have the glands of the mucous and serous membranes to undergo, in order to secrete albumen ?

ANALBUMINURIA.

As every thesis in the organismus possesses an antithesis, as globulosis and leucæmia, as fibrinosis and hyperinosis, so we may put up Analbuminuria in opposition to Albuminuria. During the continuance of hydrops the blood turns poor, even the already abnormal function of the kidney becomes worse and only a trickling through takes place of an analbuminous, alkaline fluid with a surplus of soluble or insoluble phosphoric salts, mixed with oxalic lime, coloring and extractive matters, more on account of the relative pressure than functional, i. e. the renal substance (also the heart, the brain etc.) is more or less so degenerated and atrophied, that it only acts mechanically, the vessels exert no counterpressure and a portion of easily permeable matter on account of the badly nourished nerves, etc., easily trickles through, finally in cardiac disease the transudation becomes limited to glomeruli.* It is therefore clear, how Darwall could report a case of M. B. without albuminuria, we also find in rare cases an uræmia without ammonia in the urine, but not in the vomited matter nor in the expired air. Several conditions, simultaneously acting for a long time, hasten this unfavorable state, as hypertrophy of the

---

* This is also the chief cause for the supposition, that the Malpighian tufts produce no albumen.

left heart, hence M. B., hence dropsy and a continued use of Squills.   Other diuretics act equally unfavorable, they sometimes diminish the œdema, but also the already limited functional power of the kidneys and on the whole aggravate the state.   Great thinness of the heart with irregular contraction, hence loss of energy in the circulation in general produces the same deleterious result, as we find under such circumstances a pneumonia ending fatally, when Arsenic fails to relieve.   Our patients lay great stress on the dropsy and frequently use in private practice diuretics without the knowledge of the physician, and thus shorten their own life.

The difference between albuminosis and analbuminosis will be still clearer, when we adduce the chemical qualities of the blood : in the first case the serum is diminished or indifferent, in the second increased, in the former albumen and solid serous matter increased, in the latter diminished ; in albuminosis sugar and bilious matter present, in the other urea and carbonate of Ammonia.

LOCALITY OF ALBUMINOUS SECRETION.

The question is not yet solved, in which part of the kidneys the albumen is secreted. We give a plausible view of it : In acute albuminous disease the glandular cells of the tubuli uriniferi are expelled and a large part of the gland bereft of its secreting surface or as in uræmic intoxication first paralyzed, therefore diminution of the constituents of the urine, and simultaneously, as the blood of the capillaries has no cells a stream of albumen is introduced by simple transudation in the canals, devoid of cells, or they become morbidly affected from causes already mentioned, with deficient nutrition—mostly fatty infiltration—and thus by their qualitative composition change the process of secretion. The expulsion of the surface of the glands takes place gradually, in uræmia only after the paralysis of the nerves of the capillaries is removed; the disorganization of the surface of the glands is also a gradual process in albuminuria; the more the latter progresses, the more surface is gained for the transudation, the more albumen, the less urea. When a surplus of salts, especially of insoluble phosphoric salts is secreted, no albumen will be excreted. *Analbuminuria.*

As from the large secreting surface of the kidney with its tortuous tubuli uriniferi only a portion of it is synchronically concerned in the excretion of the urinary constituents, we may now understand, why with even a far progressed organic change, as in renal suppuration, normal quantities of urea may be found with albumen, whenever a part of the kidney remains able to perform its function* and thus an accumulation of urea in the blood is prevented. According

---

* A remnant of kidney may remain able to perform its function. An old man of 78 died from suppuration of the kidney, left side except the fascia no substance, right side less than a third. And still renal secretion and no water in any cavity.

to this explanation the Malpighian tufts do not take part in the excretion of Albumen.

According to Frerichs, exudation may take place from two portions of the capillary vascular system, from the glomeruli and from the capillaries, surrounding the tubuli uriniferi. The exudation is mostly limited to the glomeruli, the Albuminates therefore only reach to the urinary canals, whereas the interstitial tissues remain free. Still there is no doubt, that under certain circumstances even those capillaries, which surround the urinary canals, may partake in the exudation.

STATISTICS.

The following compositions, which are rarely found alone, but mostly two or three together, show, how albuminuria becomes a part and parcel of renal degeneration, and what else the disease causes and draws in its circle. There were found in 74 cases : gout 2 times, herpes exedens 1, neuralgia of the nerves of the head (trigeminus and occipitalis) 1, headache as of light uræmia 1, epilepsy 1, daily epistaxis 1, cancer of the nose 1, polypus of the nose (probably accidental) 1, pulmonary tubercles 1, wasted tubercles 1, subacute pulmonary œdema 1, singultus for seven years 1, sinewy degeneration of the diaphragm 1, thin walls of the heart 3, valvular insufficiency 6, hypertrophy of the left heart 20, concentric hypertrophy 2, concentric hypertrophy and atheroma 1, atheroma 2, cardiac rheumatism 1, aneurisma aortæ 1, pancreatic disease 1, cancer of omentum 1, cancer of rectum 1, cancer of uterus 2, (Oppolzer found once M. B. in 89 cases of cancer), intestinal calculi 1, syphilitic renal degeneration 6,* renal calculi 4, fermentation of urea 2, ovarian cysts 1, hypertrophy of prostate 1, (after gonorrhœa rectal fistulæ), psoas abscess 1, nightly cramps in the calves of the legs 3, œdema pedum 5, general dropsy 1, ascites 1, pericardial dropsy 1, emboly of the left crural artery 1, of the right 1, cutaneous gangrene near the right tibia 1, sugar 1, poisoning by phosph. 1.

PATHOLOGICAL ANATOMY.

The alterations in the kidneys and other organs, which contribute primarily or secondarily to the origin of albuminuria, are evidently the same, as in M. B. In chronic cases the muscular fibres of the heart showed remarkably weak transverse striæ under the microscope, in parts they were entirely absent and all the fibres looked peculiarly homogeneous, transparent and the muscular fibrillæ, which in the sound heart are so small, looked remarkably broad. Hypertrophy and atheroma at the same time are not rare. The glandular cells appear in albuminuria flat and polygonally pressed together, their outlines are sharp. The mass surrounding the kernel is either in larger or smaller quantities mixed with fatty drops, or they are large vesicular with clear contents.

---

* It is difficult to make a differential diagnosis between arthritic, gonorrhœic, condylomatous, etc. bases, and their combinations. The sooner we reach a diagnosis, the better will we be able to give the right remedy.

In the mode of disorganizing the kidneys syphilitic disease acts differently, without changing the result, and we must therefore devote to it a special chapter, leaving it to further studies, whether Virchow's (Archiv, 8, 143, 364) amyloid state of the kidneys, which begins at the Malpighian tufts and at the conducting arteries, which are enormously thickened and infiltrated in their walls, may not also be counted in.

MORBUS BRIGHTI SYPHILITICUS.

There is not another deleterious cause, which produces in all its dimensions so deeply penetrating changes in the urinary and other organs,[*] as especially Gonorrhœa. Let us only remember the sthenosing inflammations, the concremential neoplosmata. A medical friend of ours died from stenosis of the bile-ducts, in spite of the continued use of Carlsbad, and we saw grandchildren coming into the world with the glands of the neck so enormously swollen in consequence of the gonorrhœa of their grandfather, that there was danger of suffocation. Do we not all know gonorrhœal arthritis in the second generation, the ugly wall-like scaffolding of a gonorrhœic lung, with or without condylomata. Well, if gout and tuberculosis produce albuminuria, then we may certainly affirm the same of a specific and more intense

---

[*] A most excellent and instructive monograph is, "The Intestinal Syphilis, by Arnold Beer." One and the same process may produce gonorrhœic pulmonary tubercles, syphilitic nephritis or hepatitis, just as we know, that heroic remedies choose diverse places of deposit.

form of such a dyscrasia (Rayer, Wells, Blackall,) and it is necessary for us to study the suitable remedies for such an intense disease, because, as far as we know, it has not been done before.

PATHOLOGICAL ANATOMY.

Syphilitic degeneration has this in common, that the exudations and metamorphosis in the constituents of the tissues as well as the developing neoplasmata, always appear in small foci, although spread over the whole substance of the kidney, so that the albuminous infiltration of the parenchymatous cells, their fatty degeneration, the hyperplasia of the stroma, the formation of fat therein as well as the cellular interstitial hyperplasia, are all met in juxtaposition, and partly in microscopical limitation. Very characteristic and always present are the numerous small fatty foci, permeating the cortical substance, with the interstitial hyperplasia and the lardaceous degeneration of the blood-vessels.

The following characteristics may be observed with the naked eye. The kidneys are always enlarged, the surface is either entirely smooth, or flatly rising eminences appear, alternating with superficial indentations, so that there is a state of uniform, but coarse granulation produced. The capsule may be easily drawn off in the latter case, with a smooth surface it does not adhere at all. The color of the organs is bluish-grey, interrupted by numerous intensive yellow points, standing together in groups, whereas at single points a diffuse venous redness is found. The organs are firm, slightly doughy to the touch in spite of their consistency.

Cut through, the cortical substance appears broad, even to 4 lines; diffused through the cortex are the small yellow points in groups. The color is pale greyish-red, the Malpighian bodies appearing as large pale, shining granules.

The medullary substance in comparison with the pale cortex is of strong color, mostly bright-red with grey striæ; the glomeruli and cortical arteries take on a red color, when Iodine is dropped upon them. The microscope shows the presence of lardaceous degeneration in the vascular tufts, in the conducting arteries, sometimes also in the branches of the vasa deferentia. It also shows the enlargement of the Malpighian bodies and the integrity or only slight thickening of their capsules.

The interstices appear broader, especially in the neighborhood of the groups of fatty foci, the former contain in the smooth organs accumulations of roundish kernels and cells in separate, diffusely dispersed points, and simple sinewy hyperplasy in the smaller interstitial tissue. The transit of both interstitial alterations is frequently brought about by an accumulation of cylindrical elements, lying so closely together, that no intercellular substance can be observed.

Fat in large quantities is nearly constantly observed in the interstitial tissue, partly in the newly-formed round cells, partly in the cylindrical elements, mostly in the ramified bodies of connective tissue, here mostly in the form of large drops, which effect is brought about by the fatty metamorphosis of the epithelium of the tortuous canals.

The lardaceous degeneration of the vessels appears at a time, when the alterations in the other constituents have not yet reached their highest point. Only thus a considerable diminution of the diseased organs is prevented. *The lardaceous degeneration of the blood-vessels renders their shrinking to a certain degree impossible, as this process is deprived of any retrogressive metamorphosis.* The lardaceous vascular tufts give by their persistency a kind of support to the neighboring tissues, so that in atrophied processes only a circumscript caving-in may take place, without considerable diminution of the organ. In the few cases, where the lardaceous degenerated kidneys was of smaller size, the shrinking had already taken place, when the lardaceous formation in the blood-vessels was added to it. In lardaceous degeneration Iodine naturally shows no albumen.

DIGNITY OF THESE PHENOMENA.

We have a combination of most intensive renal diseases, especially of forms, which do not allow a reformation ; we have already mentioned this in the lardaceous degeneration of the blood-vessels ; the retrogressive metamorphosis of the cellular interstitial hyperplasy does not abate this process, there rather remains a firm, impenetrable mass between vessels and urinary canals, greatly preventing the interchange of matter, and then the parenchymatous alterations must be still added to it.

No part of the cortical substance is thus spared, we have a renal disease, which in its destructive tendencies is second to none. What presents itself in some cases as excessive shrinking, what in other cases is produced by a combination of parenchymatous and interstitial disease, is here produced by the affection of all parts of the renal substance, so that the result of the disease necessarily must be *the utmost diminution of the function of the kidney.*

In fact the patient succumbs to the disease of the kidney, and the intensity of these disturbances depends not on the lardaceous degeneration of the vessels per se, but essentially on the combination of the different processes, especially of the lardaceous degeneration with the interstitial morbid state.

When does renal syphilis develop itself? is a question of importance for the therapy; for the sooner we can make our diagnosis, the surer a cure; at a late stage we cannot promise much any more, as the organic alterations are in too large quantities and too great qualitatively. As it is certain, that syphilis may throw itself with all its force on the kidneys, the examination of the urine ought never to be neglected. There are no secondary or tertiary forms of syphilis, but the organs attacked have no phenomena or the physician comes only at a late hour to make his diagnosis, but all intensive diseases have primary, secondary and tertiary foci of localization, and the same is the case with all heroic, remedies, a physiological process, which is always too much mixed together.

DIAGNOSIS.

Albuminuria naturally has the same consequences as Bright's disease, only the organic alterations arise a great deal more slowly and its course is therefore slower, more protracted, frequently for decennia. This is also the cause, why patients neglect to call in aid at the right time, as they do not suffer much or mention every thing else but the seat of the disease or rather speak of other diseases, which show themselves more distinctly, as emphysema, hypertrophy of the pancreas, gastric troubles, spasms. With such a perfect absence of renal symptoms in protracted cases with its phenomena in the stomach or in the chest a fair diagnosis is not always found, and we have seen many patients, where they came to us, only after the disease had lasted many years. After all, how easy is the examination of the urine according to Heller, all of which has already been mentioned under M. B.

PROGNOSIS.

The prognosis turns upon the greatness of the organic alterations, but even in unfavorable cases the course is slower than in tuberculosis or carcinoma, as the former goes according to the proverb: divide et impera. Analbuminuria with coarse organic lesions is absolutely fatal. Many mechanical albuminuriæ pass off and return and the prognosis after a fair diagnosis need not be entirely unfavorable.

Moderate inflammations of serous membranes, even œdema, are removed by adjusting the right remedy to the cause of the disease.

THERAPY.

The therapy differs not from that, already given in M. B., whenever we are unable to prove a distinct noxa, among which we especially mention gonorrhœa and condylomata, whose anatomical character in the kidneys distinguishes itself thus, that the lardaceous degeneration prevents the shrinking of the organ. We will give now our small experience on this thema.

If already the diagnosis of this state encounters so many difficulties, we cannot expect to meet less in the therapy, partly from poverty in our literature, partly from the scantiness of cases in consequence of the difficult diagnosis and the meagre indications for the selection of the remedy.

Remedies, moderating the course of the disease and healing even at the beginning, are: Thuja, Sabina, Acidum nitri, Aurum, Cuprum, Arsen., Tart. emet., Lycopodium, Petroleum, Sepia, Natrum-sulph., Acid-benzoic, Kali-bichromicum. But we still miss a great deal in the elucidation of these remedies, which is necessary in the physiology of them, as well as in their chemical analysis and otherwise.

A chemical analysis of Thuja, does not exist and the few symptoms given fail to give us clear indications, and we hold therefore to the general physiological action of the remedy, which proves, that the tree of life in all its species, produces arthritic wandering pains in the sero-fibrous tissues, increased and altered secretions in the mucous membranes of the kidneys, bladder and respiratory organs, and on the skin warty excrescences. We know by analogy and induction, that the balsamic and resinous remedies, used for a long time, produce fatty degeneration of the kidneys, and of the mucous membrane of the tubuli uriniferi. Thuja may therefore act just as well in syphilitic renal degeneration, as generally in gonorrhœa and condylomata, still we cannot expect great help from the long-continued use of vegetable remedies in so intensive renal alterations.

Sabina suits women better than men. Stapf's careful proving gives an arterial congestion of the kidneys and of the uterus. Tart.-emet. follows well after these two remedies, but we would remark, that this therapy rests still on mere theoretical ground, as experience is still wanting.

We know very little what alteration Tartarus produces in the kidneys; the most outspoken and clear symptom is the hæmorrhage from the Malpighian tufts. The symptoms on the lungs and large blood-vessels prove, that Tartarus is especially thus indicated, when the respiratory organs are coaffected, the right heart affected, and the cause of the disease is based on condylomata, as clinical experience has proved.

Barlow and Soer have recommended it long ago, also Frerichs in the acute forms, though from other reasons. So much is certain, that in old sycotic cases Tartarus cannot be surpassed by any remedy, even not by Lycopodium.

7*

With the exception of the salts of Aurum and Cuprum, the latter of which is worth recommending in acute syphilitic hepatitis, and whose general indications we have already given under M. B., we must also mention Acidum nitricum, which has been used since Solon, and by which, 1843, Hansen saw good effects in 18 acute cases, of whom only two died, whereas Hasse was very unsuccessful with it.

The place where we treat of this remedy, already shows the specific relationship to the distinct adjectivum, and it must not be given as formerly, only on general principles. Characteristic hints for Acid-nitr. are : aggravation at night, thus syphilitic basis or complication, nausea, sour taste, bilious diarrhœa or constipation, *dry skin*, fever, headache, dulness of the first sound of the heart—therefore related to Arsen.—intermission of the third beat of the heart, pressure in the kidneys, muddy and foul smelling urine, œdema pedum. Considering only the renal function, Acid-nitr. in consequence of hyperæmia increases at the start the secretion of urine, the urates are separated sooner than usual, but after a while they become diminished; it increases the phosphates, the Uroxanthin, this usually first symptom of incipient M. B., finally Ammonia forms quicker in the discharged urine, and the phosphates make a sediment. There is no doubt, that uric fermentation also belongs in the circuit of this remedy.

Per analogy we may safely say, that a remedy, which proves itself as a specific in diphtheritic inflammation of the throat, of the cœcum (not of the larynx), must also be of benefit in epidemic dysentery and in badly-formed inflammation of the kidneys. We prefer Acidum-nitri to Cuprum in excessive deposition of bile-pigment in the kidneys, and hence functional suspension of the action of this organ, though it may only be a valuable intercurrent remedy, which increases reaction; at any rate its action is more versatile than that of Petroleum, whose sphere has till now not been enough valued.

Looking closer to the indications, we might say, that generally (Thuja) Tartarus acts best, when condylomata are the basis of the disease, Petroleum (also Sulphur?) when gonorrhœa; Acidum-nitri., when chancres or abuse of Mercury, may be given as intercurrent remedy in all three forms. The most thankless cases are those syphilitic troubles, which treated with Mercury and Iodine withstand every kind of treatment.

Examining the symptoms of Petroleum 400–462, we find before all fistula recti, which we can hardly imagine without preceding gonorrhœa—deposits of gonorrhœa on the rectum produce in old people *ascending* fistulæ, and after a while albuminuria—difficult micturition, red sediments in the urine with shining pellicles on the surface, a dark-brown cloud in the urine, brown extremely fœtid urine, strong ammoniacal scent of the urine, discharge of prostatic fluid. The symptoms of Petroleum are clearer than those of Thuja, but they still need some experiments on animals for their supplement.

We must also mention the anatomical symptoms

observed on animals by *Bogoslowsky*, after the use of *Argentum :* the cause of the venous stasis lies in the heart and respiratory apparatus, which become sick. The muscular fibres enlarge, become dull and covered by a quantity of granular masses,' which again disappear by the addition of acetic-acid, the transverse striation of the muscular fibres is obliterated, and frequently an enlargement of the kernels of the sarcolemma was observed, but never fatty degeneration. The epithelium of the Bellinian tubules usually is in a state of dull swelling, (dulness of their contents, increased circumference of the elements, and indistinctness of the nucleus in consequence of it,) or they pass over into a fatty degeneration. The presence of fatty granules in the cells, disappearance of the nucleus, change in dark granular pellets, resorption of fat. Albumen was demonstrated in the urine of many animals, and the medullary substance of the kidneys contained more blood than the cortical substance.

Some will miss the Iodide of potash, praised by many very highly, but we never saw any benefit from it neither here nor in syphilitic hepatitis. The practical experience, which always has rendered medicine coarse and trivial, does not amount to much, as long as the conditions are not given, through which Iodine and its preparations deserve preference to other remedies. General recommendations are generally useless, if not founded on physiological experiment and strict indications in practice. Thus and never otherwise.

Among the most troublesome symptoms of Albuminuria, sometimes also among the terminal ones, belongs in coarse organic lesions the *dropsy* (compare Analbuminuria), of which we intend to speak a few words.

HYDROPS.

Dropsy* in chronic renal degeneration, especially from coarse organic changes of the heart, first as Anasarca, then Ascites, Hydrothorax, attacking mostly both sides, finally œdema pulmonum, more rarely as exudation on the pericardium (Malmston saw it three times in 69, Bright 11 times in 100 cases) troubles the patient in such a degree, that he begs a symptomatic treatment of his physician. We all know, that dropsical exudations arise by stagnation and slackened circulation after changes have occurred in the blood-carrying organs, by diminution of the plasma from the constant loss of fibrine and albumen, we must also consider, that in obstructions of circulation in the blood-making and blood-carrying organs alterations in the tissues ensue, that the formation and carrying of the blood must become anomalous and thus the anomalous quality of the blood (inasmuch as the blood-plasma is discharged outwardly through the kidneys as albumen, and in salt-hydrates through the capillaries of the peritoneum, pleura, etc. inwardly), this preponderance of watery

---

* Christison remarks, that ¾ of the dropsies occurring in Edinburgh, are caused by renal degeneration. Forget, in Strasburg, ½, in Germany ⅔. Of 430 cases 376 were accompanied by dropsy, 54 without it. Frerichs.

constituents favors a more easy transudation of serum ;
furthermore, urea is added to the dropsical fluid ;
(Guiburt, Barlow) or instead of it, but more rarely
Carbonate of Ammonia; the largest quantity of urea
was 4, 2. p. m. (Marchand). We must also recollect
the increased porosity of the walls of the blood-vessels.
It is easily proved, that dropsy does not ensue,
because the necessary quantity of water is not
discharged from the organismus on account of the
renal disease, as such dropsies we also have witnessed
in circulatory disturbances, where normal urinary
secretion, even polyuria is present. Every physician
in good practice sees cases enough, on account of the
similarity of the causal conditions, where the dropsy
precedes the albuminuria. Albuminuria fares still
worse in its course during simultaneous polyuria or
in the presence of traces of sugar in the urine.

Renal hydrops shows especially a lesser quantity
of solids in the exudation, especially of albumen,
than other dropsies and the punctio abdominis therefore can only be recommended in most urgent cases,
as it may easily produce inflammations of the serous
membranes of the abdomen, just as scarifications may
be followed by gangrenescent erythema.

Diuretics hasten fatty degeneration and atrophy of
the kidneys, squills more than parsley, etc., etc.
Where the symptom, the dropsy, is curable, the
disease must also be curable, the dropsy therefore
can only be removed by the disease itself, except
where we wish only to act palliatively, in other cases
every physician knows, that the over-exertion of a

diseased organ necessarily limits in its after effect its already limited function. We can only recommend in such cases the lemon-cure, recommended years ago in the A. H. Z., beginning with the juice of one slice, increasing the dose daily by a slice, till surfeit sets in. We could cite many cases, where death from renal atrophy ensued soon after the forced expulsion of water, e. g. by Squills, Gentian, etc.

We recommend the following Schema: Renal anasarca: Hell., Dulc. : Arsen. in disturbances of the left, Phosph. of the right heart; for serous discharges into the chest: Bry., Colch., Ars.; into the heart: Dig., Ars., Lycop.; into the abdomen: Ars., Lycop., Aur.; from most intense hepatic affection: Cuprum, or with other words, dropsy from hypertrophy of the heart: Dig., Ars., Lyc.; from a diseased right heart: Phosph., Acid-phosph.; from catching cold: Dulc., Ars., Calc-arsenic; from hepatic troubles: Lycop., Aur., in desperate cases also Cuprum.

As the chemical examination of the urine is the only reliable means, to establish the diagnosis of M. B., let us find the differences between healthy and albuminous urine.

Constituents of normal urine.		In albuminuria, Morbus Brighti.
Specific gravity 1023,		in spite of albumen, minus.
Reaction acid,		mostly acid.
Urea,	30 %	minus.
Carbonate of Ammonia,	0	more frequent, especially in Uræmia.
Uric acid,	1 %	minus to null.
Chlorides,	5 %	normal to 0.
Sulphates,	6 %	normal.

Earth phosphates,	2 %	minus.
Alkaline phosphates,	4 %	normal to plus.
Urophæine,	11½	indifferent.
Urine indigo,	traces.	plus.
Albumen,	0	copious.
Pus,	0	frequent.
Blood,	0	frequent.
Mucus & epithelium (by the microscope),	⅓ %	copious.
Exudation cylinders from the Bellinian tubules (micr.),	0	frequent.
Fungi & infusorii (micr.)	0	mostly.

To which we add an examination of the vomited matter.

Constituents of normal vomitus.		In Cholera.	In Uræmia.
Free gastric acid.	copious.	none.	diminished.
Chlorides.	copious.	copious.	copious.
Mucus & epithelium.	copious.	mucus little, epithel. much.	copious.
Albumen,	wanting.	always traces.	rare.
Bilious matter,	wanting.	wanting.	rare.
Urea,	wanting.	traces.	copious.
Carbonic fixed alkalies,	wanting.	copious.	wanting.
Combinations of Ammonia,	wanting.	traces.	copious.
Sarcina,	wanting.	fungi.	wanting.
Water,	copious.	increased.	increased.

This short monograph thus contains most. what we know of M. B. Any one who considers the chemical explanation too trifling, may turn the whole thing round and say, this or that alteration of the nerves brings forth this certain blood-crasis, such capillary and nutritive disturbances. On account of the functional unity of the organismus, the disease may be explained both ways.

The tendency of science is at present a purely realistic one. Homœopathy certainly remains the only system of medicine resting on principles, but we may hope, that the realistic work of the 19th century has not been 'in vain, but ploughed the ground, on which the ideal seed may bring forth fruit.

Although even our school has a great work still before it, we need not fear, we must only go to work with an open hand and a strong heart. As long as the physiological school is satisfied with a mere diagnosis and an old fogy therapy, every plebeian can laugh and be his own doctor. Homœopathy surpasses all other schools in its therapeutic successes, and therefore we recommend its study to all, who seek after truth.

APPENDIX.

Buchner's " Morbus Brighti " is such a finished monograph, that we considered it wrong to interpolate any notes. Still there are some remedies which physicians of high standing recommend, and at the request of the publishers we make these addenda.

Before going into therapeutics, we may be allowed to copy the following instructions given by Dr. Joseph Kidd, in an article on Bright's disease (B. J. of H. XIII, p. 568). He says: It is clearly as much our duty to promote the elimination of the urea in one case, as to extract a foreign body in another, and help by natural means to increase the secretions, that we now find take up the actions correlative to the functions of the kidneys. In proportion to the success of our efforts in this direction, we may be enabled to prolong life, and ward off much distress and pain.

Free action of the skin above all, is most essential. The occasional use of vapor-baths at 96 to 98 degrees for five to ten minutes, and regular daily ablutions with tepid soft water and soap, followed by brisk dry friction, fulfil this most satisfactorily. The increased activity of the lungs and liver, we must seek to promote by regular exercise in the open air (in dry elevated situations if possible). The action of Hepar and Terebinthina also aids us in this. A change to an equable warm dry climate (as to Egypt, Malta or Malaga,*) is of vast moment, and if the disease is of recent origin, may completely cure it. Increasing the action of the skin, it also enables the patient to take open air exercise all through the

---

* Southern California fulfils the same indications for the U. S.

winter, wonderfully exhilarates the spirits and increases the appetite.

It is also of great moment to supply abundantly all the elements, which are being carried out in excess, by the use of unstimulating albuminous and farinaceous food, in the form most easy of digestion, milk, eggs, fowl, fish, mutton, beef, peas, beans, bread, biscuits, cocoa, tea. Also a very little fresh vegetable, and ripe fruit every day.

The use of alcoholic fluids in albuminuria dependent on degeneration of the kidney, requires great tact and judgment. In that called the fatty or enlarged kidney, they are borne very well if moderately used at meals only, but in the cases of granular degeneration they aggravate the urea poisoning, and tend to cause effusion on the brain and spine (serous apoplexy). Still in many cases the patients cannot do without their accustomed stimulus. In such cases good Bordeaux wine is the least objectionable. Burgundy, or pale Sherry comes next, if necessity does not oblige pale ale or porter to be taken.

When dropsy is increasing in the extremities or in the chest, much aid will be found from brisk friction or shampooning *downwards*. This aids in the more rapid exhalation outwards through the skin of the urea-laden serum, and also seems to cause its more rapid reabsorption into the vessels in a state quickly eliminated. From this I have seen most rapid diminution of dropsy, which, though temporary, yet afforded much relief to the urgent dyspnoea and to cramps in the limbs.

In studying Hale's new remedies and others, like Apis, Nitrate of Uranium and several which are put down by different authors, as effective for albuminuria, we find that most of them produce primarily diabetes, and Niemeyer (g. e. II. 876.) also considers chronic parenchymatous nephritis, which causes the albuminuria to arise frequently, in consequence of the continued irritation of the kidneys by the saccharine secretion, forming an analogon to the balanitis, witnessed in glycosuria.

Marcy recommends *Apis mellifica* in incipient Bright's disease, in inflammation of the neck of the bladder and in *irritable bladder*. Acute œdema is the characteristic of Apis, and it acts well wherever the blood appears poisoned and the constitution depressed. Thus we find it acting beneficially in diphtheritis, in angina with general swelling and puffiness, in erysipelas and carbuncles, in variola, scarlatina, etc. We thus easily understand, that it must act beneficially in post-scarlatinal dropsy, as the infection with scarlatina poison constantly also produces alteration in the fauces and in the kidneys. During most epidemics it may only consist of simple hyperæmia, but in malignant cases disturbances of nutrition in these organs are of greater severity, and instead of simple catarrh of the fauces we find diphtheritis developed, and instead of a simple renal hyperæmia acute M. B. (Niemeyer II, 10). Apis also seems to affect more the surface, than the parenchyma of organs, and we do not therefore expect any aid from it in parenchymatous nephritis, in hepatic cyrrhosis, or in chronic cardiac troubles, but where ascites, hydrothorax, hydropericardium and anasarca are sequels of slow inflammatory states with deficient power of absorption, Apis will restore that deficiency and increased urination will be the consequence with relief of all symptoms.

We agree with Marcy and Peters (N. A. J. of H., Vol. VI. p. 486 M. M.) that *Apocynum cannabinum* is utterly useless in Bright's disease, as albuminuria was never present in any case, where the Indian hemp removed the dropsy. It may undoubtedly remove the mechanical obstacles, and thus increase the flow of urine, but only at the cost of increased degeneration in the structure of the organs affected in M. B.

Hale in his "New Remedies" mentions *Caulophyllum* and *Chimaphila* among remedies for albuminuria, but he fails to show their action in M. B. The former can be entirely dismissed, and the Prince's Pine causes mucous sediment to disappear from the urine (vesical catarrh), but any action of it on the kidneys remains more than doubtful.

The urine of *Eupatorium purpureum* shows a high specific gravity (1010, 1026, 1030,) and the characteristic constituents of the urine are not changed as proven by examination, except by the addition of *mucus*, which had increased in quantity. (Hale's N. R. p. 365). Hale considers it primarily homœopathic to diabetes insipidus, as we find among its symptoms: profuse urination, dull aching pains in renal region, a feeling as if falling toward the left, impotence; (Grauvogl considers Argentum indicated, and the disease is probably situated in the immediate neighborhood of the vagus and acusticus), and secondarily in affections of the urinary organs with scanty urine, dropsy, but Dr. P. H. Hale acknowledges, that in his case no organic disease of the heart, kidneys or liver could be discovered, and we may therefore also dismiss the Queen of the Meadow as a remedy in chronic Bright's disease, where the specific gravity is very low (even to 1005); still Hering's symptoms 145–150 and 200–227, recommend it in dropsy based on a rheumatic or rather gouty diathesis, and hence under such conditions it will aid us in removing many of the troublesome symptoms.

Helonias dioica, like *Uranium nitricum* produce primarily diabetes, and M. B. might secondarily arise from the continual drain which the system undergoes. The eclectic Paine says, that Helonias produces irritation of the urethra, pain in the kidneys, followed by albuminuria, indicating congestion, and large discharges of urine, with slightly increased specific gravity, but as the urine was not tested for albumen, we surmise, that the urine rather contained mucus instead of albumen. Hale (N. R. 532) thinks, that by hyperstimulation it may produce a congestive albuminuria, especially as we find characteristic of the remedy weariness and weight in the region of the kidneys, general weariness, and it may be therefore of benefit in post scarlatinal dropsy (it would hardly respond to M. B. from Cholera-typhoid), as such cases are due to an asthenic state of the system (p. 534), which Helonias might improve, if the symptoms correspond. Other cases mentioned show its value in melituria. E. T. Blake, M. D., has given us a monograph on *Uranium nitricum*, and cases are cited by many observers, which show its value in glycosuria. Blake doubts its beneficial action, in the removal of the sugar from the urine, but considers it especially indicated in those morbid states, comprehensively classed under the title of M. B. It is strongly indicated in the earlier stages of the small, gouty or contracting kidney, more especially where severe gastric disturbance complicates the case, and also for the irritable condition of the renal plexus of the sympathetic, inducing diuresis. Among its symptoms we find : (49) desire to urinate again immediately after voiding bladder ; (50) Chlorides increased ; all other constituents remain unchanged, (60) stiffness in loins, (70) extreme languor with fishy odor of urine, (72) debility and cold feeling with vertigo, (55) urinary tenesmus.

We consider symptom 50 of great importance in M. B., as Niemeyer (II, 22) remarks, that in dropsical patients the chlorides of the blood pass in large quantities over into the dropsical exudations. Its importance is explained by the fact, that in such patients, as long as the dropsy increases, the urine contains very little chlorides, but that the dropsy will steadily diminish, as soon as the chlorides are discharged with the urine in a quantity far surpassing its norm (Vogel, Liebermeister).

Dr. Mayer Baruch, of New York, considers *Kalmia latifolia* a remedy, too much neglected in albuminuria. Bayes, (Applied Homœopathy, p. 108,) finds it indicated in rheumatic neuralgic pains, most severe at night, precluding sleep and to the sensation of the patient the pains appear to be in the bones, probably in the periosteum. Dr. Pretsch, (A. H. R. I, 325,) recommends it in those cases of rheumatism, where the pains shift about from one place to another. Hering says : in disease of the heart, which alternate with rheumatism or have originated in rheumatic attacks, kalmia must become most important, as there is no medicine in the whole Materia Medica, which has such control over the pulse, except Digitalis; (we may say therefore with Buchner, all remedies, which disturb the arterial circulation in such a high degree, may also produce renal degeneration, or at least albuminuria, Vide Digitalis p. 75). We also know, that frequent exposure to cold and wet is a principal cause of acute as well as of chronic M. B., and as it corresponds to the great family of diseases, which we comprise under the collective names of rheumatismus and gout, particularly to that class, which belongs to the North, we consider the mountain-laurel a remedy undeservedly neglected in many cases, and we would recommend a reproving of it to our provers' unions.

We come now to the poke-weed, a regular polychrest. *Phytolocca decandra* we have just begun to study and it has not yet received its just place in our Materia Medica. Bayes (l. c. p. 139), found Phytolocca of service in diphtheria and fatty degeneration, both diseases characterised by very feeble performance of nerve function and by a tendency to failure of the heart's action. His confrére Hughes (Pharmacodynamic, p. 460,) praises it as an accession to our means of combating chronic rheumatism, not only periosteal (kalmia, mezereum,) but its influence extends also to the other fibrous tissues, as the sheaths of nerves and the fasciæ (Rhus). It has also cured syphilitic rupia (Br. J. xxvi, 327) and syphilitic ulcers of the feet (ibid 488.) Our own Burt in his provings of the poke-root shows, that his urine was at first diminished, afterwards increased. The urine remained acid and became decidedly albuminous, as proved by the usual tests, and its specific gravity greatly increased. It may therefore become a valuable remedy in acute Bright's disease, especially whenever the system is prostrated by a zymotic poison, but also in chronic albuminuria it deserves consideration, should further studies prove that fatty degeneration belongs to it.

Peters (Hom. Examiner, new series, 285) introduced *Merc.*

cor. in the armamentarium for Bright's disease. He shows, that in every case of poisoning by the corrosive, albumen was found in the urine, and the kidneys, especially the cortical substance, enlarged, soft and flabby and of a marbled appearance. Cold, poverty and exposure are the most frequent sources of M. B. and the action of Mercury also predisposes to cold and rheumatism. The concomitant diseases of granular kidney (Prout) are the same, as we find them from improper exposure while under the influence of Mercury, as dropsy, dyspepsia and chronic vomiting, diarrhœa, pleurisy and peritonitis, catarrh and pneumonia, cerebral symptoms and coma, rheumatism, organic diseases of the heart or liver. Teste (Materia Medica, 144) found the corrosive useful in melituria as well as in albuminuria, in impotence especially from onanism, in hæmoptysis with a dry cough, violent dyspnœa and burning heat in the chest, in acute and chronic articular rheumatism, etc. Headland says of the mercurials, that they deprive the blood of one-third of its fibrin, one-seventh of its albumen, one-third or more of its globules and at the same time load it with a fetid fatty matter, the product of decomposition. Brodies' and Orfila's experiments also show the paralyzing influence, which the corrosive Mercury exerts on the heart and its secondary action on lungs and kidneys, but so far we need yet an explanation of the action of this penetrating poison, and this may be the reason, why Buchner excludes it from his therapeutics.

Some minor remedies might still be mentioned, but after all we must strictly individualize every case and every remedy and thus many a cure will reward the diligent student, and whenever a cure is not possible any more, we may be still enabled to prolong life and to make the passing years more comfortable to the weary traveler.

RECENT
HOMŒOPATHIC PUBLICATIONS

Sent Post-paid on receipt of Price. Address any
Homœopathic Pharmacy or the Publishers direct:

BOERICKE & TAFEL,
145 Grand Street, New York.

Annual Record of Homœopathic Literature 1870.
Edited by C. G. Raue, M. D. 496 Pages. 8vo. $3.50.

☞ In the preparation of the ANNUAL RECORD, Professor RAUE
has been assisted by an able corps of collaborators, and no labor
or expense has been spared to have the whole a complete *digest
of all the valuable information* scattered throughout the periodical
literature of Homœopathy, during the year 1869. The Journals
of the UNITED STATES, ENGLAND, GERMANY, FRANCE, SPAIN, and
other countries, have furnished materials fot this great work.

Annual Record of Homœopathic Literature, 1871.
Edited by C. G. Raue, M. D. 255 Pages. 8vo. $2.50.
N. B. The third Vol. will soon be in the printer's hands.

☞ The arrangement of the work is the same as that of last
year. Dr. C. Hering has arranged the part on Materia Medica,
Dr. T. F. Allen, the chapter on the eye, Dr. M. McFarlan, the
surgical part, and the rest by Dr. C. G. Raue. There is no
Appendix to this volume.

Baehr, Dr. B. The Science of Therapeutics, according
to the Principles of Homœopathy, by B. BAEHR, M. D.
Translated and enriched with numerous additions from
Kafka and other sources. By C. J. Hempel, M. D. 2 vols.
1,387 pages. Royal 8vo. $10.00.

☞ This work is to take the place of the late Hartmann's Acute
and Chronic Diseases, but in point of scientific value and practical usefulness, it is far superior to the former. Dr. Hempel
has incorporated large sections from Kafka in the same, has
also on suitable occasions introduced the new remedies and has
made valuable additions from our Journals and his personal
records.

Bell, Dr. Jas. B. The Homœopathic Therapeutics of Diarrhœa, Dysentery, Cholera, Cholera morbus, Cholera infantum and all other loose evacuations of the Bowels. 168 pages. Bound in Muslin. 12mo. $1.25.
Interleaved with writing paper, half morocco. $2.25.

Berjeau, J. Ph. The Homœopathic Treatment of Syphilis, Gonorrhœa, Spermatorrhœa and Urinary Diseases. Revised with numerous additions. By J. H. P. Frost, M. D. 256 pages. 12mo. $1.50.

Boenninghausen, Dr. C. Therapeutic Pocket Book for Homœopathic Physicians, to be used at the bedside of the Patient and in Studying the Materia Medica Pura. 510 pages. 8vo. $3.00.

Breyfogle, Dr. W. L. Epitome of Homœopathic Medicines. 383 pages. 12mo. $1.50.
Interleaved with writing paper, half morocco. 18mo. $3.00.

☞ This work differs from other Epitomes, in treating of a larger number of remedies, and in the arrangement of its material in comparative form. The leading symptoms of all well-established provings are here arranged in as concise form as possible.

Burt, Dr. W. H. Characteristic Materia Medica. 460 pages. 12mo. $3.00.
Interleaved with writing paper, half morocco. $5.00.

☞ In this work the author gives the *characteristic symptoms* or key-notes of two hundred and three remedies, and has adopted the method of grouping those remedies which produce similar physico-pathological and pathogenetic symptoms.

Hale, Dr. E. M. Lecture on Diseases of the Heart. In three Parts. Part I. Functional Diseases of the Heart. Part II. Inflammatory Affections of the Heart. Part III. Organic Diseases of the Heart. 206 pages. 8vo. $2.00.

Jahr, Dr. G. H. G. Therapeutic Guide; the most important results of more than Forty Years' Practice, with personal observations regarding the truly reliable and practically verified curative indications in actual cases of disease. Translated with Notes and New Remedies. By C. J. Hempel, M. D. 364 pages. 8vo. $3.50.

Jahr, Dr. G. H. G. Clinical Guide or Pocket Repertory for the Treatment of Acute and Chronic Diseases. Translated by C. J. Hempel, M. D. Second American revised and enlarged Edition, from the third German Edition, enriched by the Addition of the New Remedies. By S. Lilienthal, M. D. 624 pages. 12mo. $3.00.

Jahr, Dr. G. H. G. The Venereal Diseases, their Pathological Nature, correct Diagnosis, and Homoeopathic Treatment. Prepared in accordance with the Author's own as well as with the experience of other Physicians, and accompanied with critical Discussions. Translated, with numerous and important additions from the works of other authors, and from his own experience. By C. J. Hempel, M. D. 428 pages. 8vo. $4.00.

Index to the first eighteen volumes of the North American Journal of Homoeopathy. 8vo. $2.00.

Laurie, Dr. J. The Homoeopathic Domestic Medicine. First American from the twenty-first English edition. Edited and revised, with numerous important additions, and the introduction of the new remedies, by R. I. McClatchey, M. D. 1034 pages. 8vo. $5.00.

☞ The merits of "Laurie's Homoeopathic Domestic Medicine" are best attested by the popularity of the work in Great Britain, where upwards of 21,000 copies have been sold to the most intelligent portion of the community, and in this country the work ran through three editions in the first year.

Lippe, Dr. A. Text Book of Materia Medica, 714 pages. 8vo. $6.00.

☞ This work contains the characteristic and most prominent symptoms of two hundred and ten remedies. It has been introduced into our colleges as a Text Book and was very favorably received by the profession.

Lord, I. S. P. On Intermittent Fever, and other Malarious Diseases. 341 Pages. 8vo. $3.00.

☞ In an introduction of forty-seven pages, the author lays down his theory, and substantiates his views by a record of two hundred and fifteen cases of ague, of all kinds, giving their treatment, and a running commentary thereon. To these a very copious double index—one to the remedies and the other to the symptoms—serves as a concordance.

Raue, Dr. C. G. Special Pathology and Diagnosis, with Therapeutic Hints. 644 pages. Extra 8vo. $5.00.

☞ This standard work is used as a Text Book in all our colleges, and is found in almost every physician's library. An especially commendable feature is, that it contains the application of nearly all the *new remedies* contained in Dr. Hale's work on Materia Medica.

Raue, Dr. C. G. Annual Record of Homœopathic Literature, 1870. 496 pages. 8vo. $3.50.

Raue, Dr. C. G. Annual Record of Homœopathic Literature, 1871. 8vo. $2.50.

Complete list of BOERICKE & TAFEL's Homœopathic Publications will be furnished free on application. Address:

BOERICKE & TAFEL, HOMŒOPATHIC PHARMACY,

145 *Grand St., New York.*